THE OUTLAW OF SHERWOOD FOREST

BY JOHN SEVEN

capstone
young readers

The Time-Tripping Faradays
are published by Capstone Young Readers
A Capstone Imprint
1710 Roe Crest Drive
North Mankato, Minnesota 56003
www.capstoneyoungreaders.com

Library of Congress Cataloging-in-Publication Data
Seven, John, author.
  The outlaw of Sherwood Forest / by John Seven; illustrated by Stephanie
Hans.
      pages cm. -- (The time-tripping Faradays; [4])
  Summary: Their latest adventure takes teenagers Dawkins and Hypatia
back to thirteenth-century Nottingham and Sherwood Forest, but when
they find a time-traveling device in a cave they find themselves far in the
future—and closer to the forces that are tampering with time.
  ISBN 978-1-4342-9174-5 (library binding) -- ISBN 978-1-62370-111-6
(paper over board) -- ISBN 978-1-4342-9176-9 (pbk.) -- ISBN 978-1-4965-
0102-8 (ebook)
1. Time travel--Juvenile fiction. 2. Brothers and sisters--Juvenile fiction.
3. Conspiracies--Juvenile fiction. 4. Adventure stories. 5. Sherwood
Forest (England)--Juvenile fiction. 6. Great Britain--
History--13th century--Juvenile fiction. [1. Time travel--Fiction. 2. Brothers
and sisters--Fiction. 3. Secrets--Fiction. 4. Adventure and adventurers--
Fiction. 5. Science fiction. 6. Sherwood Forest (England)--
Fiction. 7. Great Britain--History--13th century--Fiction.] I. Hans,
Stephanie, illustrator. II. Title.
  PZ7.S51450u 2014
  813.6--dc23
                          2014001810

Cover illustration: Stephanie Hans
Designer: Kay Fraser
Photo-Vector Credits: Shutterstock

Printed in China by Nordica
0414/CA21400608
032014   008120NORDF14

FOR HARRY AND HUGO

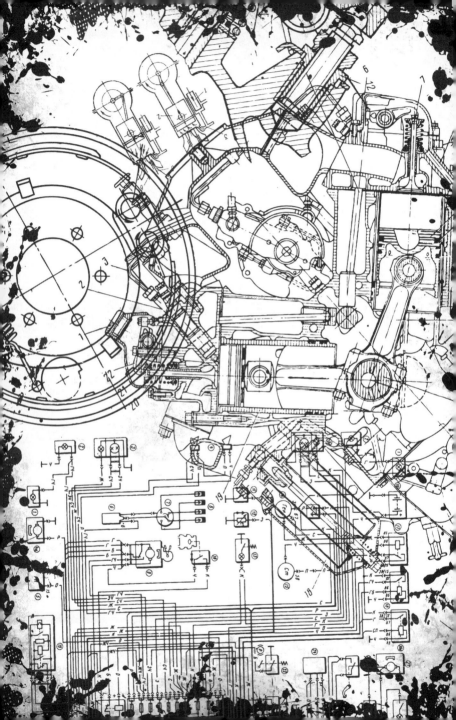

CHAPTER

1

What always seemed to get Dawk and Hype Faraday into trouble was the fact that they were time travelers.

Their parents were temporal researchers. Some temporal researchers studied the history of weaponry. Some studied war. Others studied deadly extinct animals. Abul and Zheng Faraday studied the history of footwear. Their employer, the Cosmos Institute, located in a huge building called the Alvarium in the twenty-fifth century, was interested in everything. So the Faradays were official, specially trained time travelers. But that didn't really keep their children out of trouble.

In fact, trouble seemed to follow Dawk and Hype Faraday around.

At that very moment, they were somewhere in Peru. It was the year 200 AD, and they were in a worship chamber filled with huge jugs and bowls and all sorts of pottery. The chamber was inside a mud pyramid. In the heat and humidity of the Peruvian summer, the coolness of the mud pyramid was partly a relief.

But what wasn't a relief? Being surrounded by the followers of the High Priestess of the Moche civilization, all of whom were chattering with excitement. And it didn't help that the siblings from the far-flung future were currently tied to a sacrificial altar, with a giant crab-like thing called Ai Apaec preparing to bite off their heads.

They were managing to stay relatively calm, but tension was rising.

I'm sure that's a FleshBot and not a real giant crab monster. (Hype)

Well, of course it's a FleshBot, but that doesn't mean

it isn't a real giant crab monster and it won't bite our heads off. It's a head-eating FleshBot! (Dawk)

Dawk and Hype were communicating via the Link, the neural network that let them talk with each other, their friends, and anyone else who was connected.

You might be interested to know that Ai Apaec translates to "decapitator," which doesn't waste any time explaining the monster's main talent. (Fizzbin)

Fizzbin was their computer-generated escort back in the twenty-fifth century. Dawk and Hype were hopeful that he could get them out of the trouble they were currently in.

I just shot Mom a message that we'll be late for dinner. (Hype)

Ai Apaec continued to inch toward the altar, a construction of carved stones embedded in the mud walls.

Ai Apaec was the third killer monster they had faced in as many weeks, and Dawk and Hype were completely exhausted.

Whether the monster was a real living creature or a high-tech construction that just looked real—a

FleshBot—didn't matter at this point. The giant crab came closer. It was inches away from Dawk's head. The world's slowest monster, perhaps, but that didn't make Dawk and Hype feel any safer.

Fizzbin, is there a plan for Benton to snap us up and save my head? (Dawk)

He's waiting until the pivotal moment when Ai Apaec goes for your head in order to get an accurate measurement on the bio-robotics of its jaws. Not much is known about crab mouths, let alone FleshBot crab mouths. Don't worry, you will de-materialize out of here before the fangs snap around your skull. (Fizzbin)

Great! (Dawk)

. . . I think . . . (Fizzbin)

Ai Apaec's jaws opened wide above the boy's head, and that one moment seemed to last an eternity. Dawk felt all swimmy, like he was trapped in waves but they were made out of air instead of water.

Then he realized that the time-travel process had begun. Time was breaking down around him. He could just make out Ai Apaec's razor-sharp fangs when . . .

Slowly . . .

Benton's lab in the twenty-fifth century materialized around him and his sister. Mom and Dad were already there.

"I knew you wouldn't lose your heads," Dad said.

His sense of humor was like that.

CHAPTER

2

Once Dawk and Hype had a moment to catch their breath in the twenty-fifth century, they were barraged with questions about how they had ended up nearly being eaten alive. Fizzbin had relayed the information back to the twenty-fifth century, but it hadn't all been analyzed. Benton, who oversaw all the time-traveling missions out of the Alvarium, was insistent that he needed to hear Dawk and Hype's version of the events.

You would think a large crustacean mere moments from tearing off Dawk's head is a very horrible thing to happen, but there were even more frightening discoveries in ancient Peru. (Fizzbin)

"Yeah," Hype said. "Like telephones, for example."

"Telephones?" Benton asked.

"They're like NeuroNet, but with handles and dials and wires and stuff," Dawk said.

"I'm sure Benton knows what telephones are," said Mom.

"I do. But I can't begin to imagine what they were doing in ancient Peru," Benton said.

The ancient Peruvian telephone system was still under construction, but the plans we uncovered had it stretching to points north and south in order to reach across the continent and provide communication between far-flung inhabitants at the time. (Fizzbin)

"About 1600 years before phones should have existed," Hype added. "Telephones weren't even invented until the 1870s."

Hype explained her theory. If a network of instantaneous communication was created between tribes throughout early South America, it would also create a union of tribal culture.

By the time Europeans showed up a thousand years later, they would encounter a well-organized group of allied countries. This would have changed history — Europe would not slowly invade the Americas as it was recorded in the Alvarium's history banks. Instead, the united Native Americans would have defeated them and maybe even considered sailing eastward to conquer Europe.

"From what I've seen in NeuroPedia, that wouldn't be the worst thing to happen," Hype finished.

But as Hype knows, we are not here to judge history right or wrong in these cases, we are only here to preserve what already happened. (Fizzbin)

"Too bad," Hype added.

Hype was very clever, though. She thought of breaking into the central temple to disrupt the telephone network there. (Fizzbin)

"But the High Priestess caught us trying and offered our heads to the crab FleshBot," Dawk said. "We're pretty sure the High Priestess was Antevorta, the fake goddess from the future whom we met in ancient Rome."

"She kept telling the Moche guards that were in the temple that she was going to finish delivering 'the gift of traveling voices' that had been given to her by the gods," Hype said.

Benton was quiet for a moment, taking in all the information before he spoke.

"This seems to point directly at the mysterious time traveler — or travelers — from the future tampering with the past," he said finally. "Who else would be capable of creating a telephone system in ancient South America? Surely that time traveler is behind this."

"Alexander Graham Bell could have," Dawk said. "If he had an interpreter. And a time machine."

"Who's Alexander Graham Bell?" Hype asked.

"Finally, something I know that you don't!" Dawk said, smiling.

Never mind all that. I am currently sending a visual to everyone in the room through the Link. I believe it will be especially of interest to Benton. (Fizzbin)

The visual appeared in each person's NeuroCache. Fizzbin had sent them an image of a beautifully created and painted pot, spinning slowly so that it could be seen from all vantage points. The pot's designs were very complex.

If you look closely, you will notice this ancient Moche artifact currently in the Alvarium holdings has very complicated marks all over it. My analysis reveals these to be the plans for the very telephone network we are speaking of. Other Moche ceramics in the Heritage Vault seem to contain plans for building the actual telephones. (Fizzbin)

"Well, it seems I need to call up some of these from the vault and get them analyzed," Benton said. "I also need to thank Dawk for his patience in regard to his head. I'm positive that the data we got from his near-decapitation will help us out in some way in the future. Maybe." Benton smiled.

"What with the telephone mess in ancient Peru, you'll probably need some crafty troubleshooters to go take care of the clean-up," Dad said. He glanced over at Mom. "I wonder what our schedule looks like."

"Don't you worry," Benton said, patting Abul Faraday on the shoulder. "I wouldn't throw you into that mess again. The Faraday family is headed for

England in 1267. Much less stressful. You can really get down to work there."

"Is there anything interesting in 1267?" asked Dawk.

Benton nodded happily. "Shoes! And lots of them!"

CHAPTER 3

Dawk and Hype were glad to be on another mission. Since they first began accompanying their parents on historical research into the past, normal life had become, well, boring . . . as well as depressing.

The Alvarium, where the remainder of twenty-fifth-century humanity lived, felt like a ghost town; so many of its citizens now spent their leisure hours PlayModding.

Playing thousands of highly complex and detailed virtual games made the citizens seem, outwardly at least, catatonic, and definitely not much fun to be with.

Even in the huge space called the Mall in the center of the Alvarium, the only people there were stretched out in the seating areas, PlayModding and tuned out from their surroundings.

It was particularly depressing to Hype that her best friend, Ezrine, had become so obsessed with playing. Whenever Hype tried to talk with her, Ezrine never stopped multi-Playmodding in her mind, which was the latest fad, a blank stare and an empty smile greeting her former friend.

And so Dawk and Hype had no complaints about heading to England in 1267.

The first thing Dawk noticed about 1267 was all the mud. This was also the second and third thing he noticed about 1267 as well—there was just so much of it everywhere. Horses, wagons, people, houses, everything seemed covered with it. And it smelled.

Maybe it wasn't just mud.

I could get an analysis through the OpBot for you. *(Fizzbin)*

No, thanks. It's probably better not to know. (Dawk)

The biggest challenge was figuring out what to do every day. Pretty often, like today, Dawk just had no idea how to spend his time while his parents were learning the mysteries of thirteenth-century footwear.

He usually spent as much time in Nottingham Castle as he could, mostly to avoid the mud. That was fine, but it had a downside as well. Benton had secured positions for his parents at the court of Reginald Grey, the constable of Nottingham Castle, and he wasn't so bad, but his associates there— the Sheriff of Nottinghamshire and Derbyshire, Simon de Hedon, and his under-sheriff, Hugo de Babington—were very, very annoying.

And nastier than the mud.

Once, Dawk had witnessed de Hedon and de Babington demanding a tankard of mead from one of the castle servants. Then, in the company of their friend Constable Grey, de Hedon had complained about the wooden tankard, gone on and on about how a castle as fine as his needed pewter, and then said he'd prefer some English wine instead. He chuckled and said, "Who needs food or drink from France?"

Then he and de Babington threw their tankards against the wall. They repeated that four or five times, and a poor servant had to run and swiftly bring the two guests new wine each time. Grey just watched with a grim smile on his lips and said nothing. Finally, de Hedon launched into a story about how de Babington had forced widows and orphans to pay a special widow and orphan tax that day. Or maybe that had been a joke. Dawk wasn't entirely sure. But they made hanging out in the castle not so great.

Maybe going out into the muddy world isn't such a bad thing. The inside of this place makes me feel dirtier than the mud all over town. (Dawk)

When he was in the mood, Dawk spent time with Hype, going through the castle collections in the archive. The archive was really a huge, locked room piled with all sorts of art and manuscripts and souvenirs from other lands. Probably stuff that had been either stolen or won in battles.

There was always the option of a PlayMod.

The hot one at the moment was Robin Hood Rally. But playing that, he'd just be in a vReality version of where he already was, except with race cars. On second thought, maybe that wouldn't be so bad, racing through Nottingham at top speed. He wondered how the cars would handle in all that mud.

Do you know how stuffy it gets in here? And dusty. Meet me outside for a walk. (Hype)

Sure thing. Is your Visual Cortex Shell programmed for good boots? It's a mess out there. (Dawk)

Their VC Shells were the niftiest device that temporal researchers used on their trips. Light waves around the time travelers were altered so that viewers outside the Shells, meaning everyone the time travelers met, would see whatever they were programmed to see. Dawk and Hype had programmed their shells to project appropriate thirteenth-century English clothing. It saved the Faradays from carrying extensive wardrobes during their expeditions. And it was cheaper.

But the VC Shells merely created an illusion, not a barrier. They didn't prevent the Faradays from experiencing the real world in all its three dimensions and five senses.

❧

The air around town smelled bad. Very bad. And nothing protected the Faraday nostrils from the glory that was Nottingham.

This isn't really what I was thinking of when I thought I'd get out for some fresh air. (Hype)

OpBot analysis reveals this atmosphere to be much cleaner than what you have breathed in other travels. (Fizzbin)

There's no accounting for an OpBot's sense of smell, I guess. (Dawk)

There were all sorts of things contributing to the stench. Animals roamed freely—in stalls, on the muddy pathways, in homes—and none of them cared where they went to the bathroom.

Butchers had meat out for sale that did not look like anything you would want to stick in your mouth, ever. Flies covered the meat, and Dawk noticed other gross ooglies here and there. People would handle the meat with the ooglies on it, and then pick up vegetables afterward, throwing it all in their sacks.

I don't think I really appreciated the tidy eras we've visited. Even the Neanderthals were cleaner than this. (Dawk)

They passed some shacks, where medicine was brewed from roots and poured into little bottles for sale. Whatever these people were cooking up added a stinging, bitter addition to the medley of stink.

Maybe if we get farther out, away from all this activity. (Hype)

And the animals. (Dawk)

Farther on, it did smell better and was actually less muddy. They were still in Nottingham, but instead of animals and butchers and medicine makers, they saw potters and glassmakers, as well as other businesses.

A soap maker! That might come in handy. (Hype)

Across the path, Dawk spotted a young woman—she didn't look much older than Hype—coming out of a wooden building. She was carrying a pile of what looked like paper, and was having difficulty walking in the slippery mud. Her pile looked like it was going to tumble over, and when a few sheets slipped onto the ground, Dawk ran over as carefully as he could to pick them up. He handed them to her but then paused.

"Maybe you don't want these dirty sheets on all your clean ones," he suggested.

The girl smiled. "If you could take those back to my shop, I'd be very grateful, sir," she said.

Dawk jogged in with the sheets and placed them on a table just inside the door. Then he went back outside.

"Do you need help with those?" Dawk asked, gesturing at the other pages.

"I'd better just go in and try to clean those sheets off," the girl said. "I don't want the order to come up short, and I'd like to not have to make anymore." She walked carefully back into her shop. "Constable Grey is a fair enough man, but even he likes his parchment orders fulfilled properly, and I don't want to get my brother in trouble for helping set me up in this business."

Dawk and Hype followed her in and watched

as she dropped her pile on the table next to the muddied sheets. The room was framed in flimsy-looking shelving that held rolls and small folded piles of parchment. There was a table at the center, with sharp-looking tools scattered around it, and an entrance to another room that was filled with small vats and piles of frames.

"You make paper?" Hype asked.

"I'm a parchment maker," the girl said, pushing straggly brown hair out of her eyes. "I specialize in goat."

"You what?" Dawk asked, confused.

"I make parchment out of goat."

Isn't parchment a kind of paper? (Hype)

A kind of goat paper, I guess. (Dawk)

Parchment was an ancient way of making writing material out of animal skin. (Fizzbin)

They write on animal skin? (Dawk)

I guess animal skin is good for more than just shoes. (Hype)

"So, all this is made out of goat?" Hype asked, looking at the sheets of parchment on the table.

"Better goat than sheep," the young woman

said. "I don't want to pay the high sheepskin tax. There will be a goatskin tax soon enough, though. They'd tax my brain for thinking if they could figure out a way to keep track of my thoughts."

As a matter of fact, in the twenty-first century—
(Fizzbin)

"I bet if they made a tax on our hands, we'd have to pay a thumb tax," Dawk said.

The girl laughed. "No one makes jokes around here anymore, so thank you for that." She held out her hand. "Godiva Godberd. Diva to my friends."

Dawk and Hype each shook her hand.

"Why don't we help you make your delivery?" Hype asked. "We're staying at the castle. Our parents are doing work with Grey."

"As long as you're not 'shamed to be seen with me around such grand, noble types as the constable," Diva said. "Don't want to taint you in the eyes of the law."

What is she going on about? (Dawk)

It's like signing on in the middle of a PlayMod . . . you're only getting half the story. (Hype)

I have done preliminary searches in the history banks

for "Diva Godberd." No mention so far, but the history banks aren't always kind to ordinary people. (Fizzbin)

"We'll take the risk," Hype told Diva.

As they trudged in the mud through the town toward the castle, Dawk and Hype noticed that the townspeople all seemed to know their new companion.

"Give your father a hug and one for yourself, dear girl!" someone yelled.

"Best to you, Diva! And a kiss for your old dad!" came another voice.

"Blessed be your father, Diva!"

Well, some people around town aren't ashamed of her. (Dawk)

"Everyone knows you!" Hype said.

"They know me," Diva said. "And they know my brother. But they know my father best."

"Is he famous?" Hype asked.

"Fought with de Montfort, didn't he?" Diva said with a shrug. "They'll not forget that."

Who is her father? (Hype)

The only de Montfort I can find significant mention of is Simon de Montfort, who rebelled against England's

King Henry III and became leader of the country for about a year until he was killed in battle. (Fizzbin)

So he was a king, too? (Hype)

No, just an earl. (Fizzbin)

I'll never get all these old-fashioned fancy titles straight. (Hype)

"Where is your father now?" Hype asked.

"He fled after Evesham. It was all a shambles then," Diva said. "Went to the forest and stayed there."

Evesham was de Montfort's final battle. Her father must have been a soldier who survived and went into hiding to escape supporters of the king. (Fizzbin)

"Do you ever see him?" Hype asked.

"Oh, yes," Diva said, "but don't breathe a word of that in the castle. They'll expect me to lead them to the notorious outlaw of Sherwood Forest, and I would die first."

Wait a second. The outlaw of Sherwood Forest? Doesn't that mean— (Hype)

I believe you know him as Robin Hood. (Fizzbin)

Her dad is Robin Hood? This trip's going to be the best one ever! (Dawk)

CHAPTER

4

As they waited for Grey in a small stone chamber inside the castle, Dawk and Hype were quiet. But on the Link, they were abuzz with what they'd learned.

I've done all the PlayMods! Robin Hood's Merry Masquerade, Robin Hood and the Terror Trees of Sherwood Forest, Robin Hood: King of Archery, Robin Hood's Ye Big Heiste. Lots more. Plus the spin-offs— Little John's Big Battle Bonanza was my favorite, but Little John: Staffmaster was pretty good, too. I love Robin Hood! (Dawk)

Then it is my misfortune to tell you that there is no

historical basis to believe Robin Hood was a real person. (Fizzbin)

PlayMods wouldn't lie! (Dawk)

I wouldn't qualify it as lying. PlayMods make up stories. Like with your favorite, Bone Man. (Fizzbin)

Bone Man is not some story. I'm convinced he really does lurk outside the Alvarium, hunting for flesh on bones. I mean, anything's possible. (Dawk)

So no time traveler has ever met Robin Hood? (Hype)

None ever. But it seems one of the prime influences for the legend is in fact Diva's father, Roger Godberd. (Fizzbin)

Never heard of him. (Dawk)

I have created a Roger Godberd entry in NeuroPedia. That will tell you everything you require. (Fizzbin)

Hype quickly read the article in the Link's ever-growing, ever-inclusive virtual encyclopedia, marveling at how quickly Fizzbin had gathered all the available data to create a public biography of Diva's father.

So technically, Robin Hood is her dad, right? I mean, if he influenced the legend, he might as well be the legend, right? (Dawk)

Hype ignored her brother, but she jumped to attention when someone entered the chamber. It wasn't Grey or his secretary, but de Babington, who had a smug smile on his face. Hype noticed that Diva's expression went blank and her body tensed up.

"The constable is occupied with more important business and asked if I would do him the service of inspecting his property," de Babington said. "Don't worry, he told me what to look for in fresh parchment. I shall be fair."

He began flipping carelessly through the piles with pursed lips, as if he were only pretending to pay attention.

"Fine, fine, fine," de Babington said. "He'll take these, but we're deducting a new tax from your payment."

"What new tax?" Diva asked.

"Outlaw tax," the under-sheriff said. "Sheriff says we have to find some way to make up for the wasted time people like your father create for us. Hunting him and his fellows in the woods. Soldiers have to be paid, horses must be fed. And besides, there are other, darker things in the forest that need attending to. Outlaw tax covers that, too."

"It's not fair," said Hype.

De Babington smiled. "The tax can be waived, however, if you can help us in other ways."

"I told you that I don't know where my father is," Diva said through gritted teeth.

"Well, should that change, report it to us," de Babington said. "Then you will be exempt from the outlaw tax. And we'll have more time for the real dangers."

Should we do something? This guy is horrible. (Hype)

I think we need to stay out of it. (Dawk)

Dawk is correct. (Fizzbin)

Hype watched as Diva stood her ground against de Babington. It was obvious that she was doing her best to remain calm but firm, and Hype marveled at how well she kept it up against a creep like de Babington.

"Here is your fee," the under-sheriff said, tossing a couple of coins on top of the parchments. "Don't let your father steal it from you."

Diva took the coins and turned to leave. Dawk

and Hype began to follow her, but stopped suddenly when de Babington spoke.

"You're the shoe people's brood," de Babington said.

"What about it?" said Dawk.

The under-sheriff shrugged. "Don't know if your parents would approve of the company you keep. That one has some questionable relations."

"Is there some friendship tax we need to worry about?" Hype asked. Then, with Dawk following close behind, she hurried to catch up with Diva.

"Don't let that guy bother you," Hype told her.

"I don't mean to," Diva explained, "but they squeeze me like a turnip till I have not a crust to my name. I wonder how long it will be before I am forced to join my father's band permanently, just to stay alive."

Dawk and Hype left Diva at her shop, but they couldn't stop worrying about her.

"We both heard him with our own ears, and

he was horrible," Hype told her parents over their afternoon meal.

"I doubt there's anything you can do," Mom said, frowning. "It's sad."

"Someone's being treated horribly, and you worry about messing up time?" Hype asked. "This is just one girl in an isolated little place! Fizzbin says she's not even in the history banks. There has to be some way to help her out without totally destroying reality!"

"That's not what I meant," said her mother. "I'm more worried that if you intervene, you might end up making life even more miserable for her."

"But they're bullying her!" Hype argued.

"It's England in 1267," Mom said. "People are bullied here all the time. It's a part of living for some people. But at least we know it gets better!"

"But it won't get better until a thousand years from now," Hype said sadly. "I don't think Diva can wait that long."

After the meal, Hype moped around, trying to figure out how to pass the time and get her mind off Diva. Going outside certainly wasn't going to do it. Other versions of the same problem were everywhere she looked. It infuriated Hype, all the injustices in the past. And there were a lot of them.

She could go to the archive. Maybe poking around there would put her mind on sillier things— because that was what it was, a dusty old collection of silly things. Amidst a few treasures, that is.

Dawk, do you want to check out the archive with me? (Hype)

I'm right in the middle of Dueling Dirigibles. (Dawk)

Okay. (Hype)

She had a sudden flash of her friend Ezrine, lying in the Mall at the Alvarium, her eyes blank, her mouth half open.

Never mind. I'll be right there. I wish I could fly a real dirigible. That's what this PlayMod is missing. (Dawk)

The real danger of crashing your dirigible? (Hype)

The real danger of flying a dirigible in Robin Hood times while trying to save history from destruction. Exactly. (Dawk)

Outside the archive, a guard had to search them before they could enter the room. Inside, as usual, were piles and piles of treasure and junk.

"Is this stuff organized?" Dawk asked.

"Supposedly," Hype said. "I haven't been able to figure it out, though."

"Look at all these crowns!" Dawk said, peering into a crate. "I wonder if these are from kingdoms that have been conquered."

"Or maybe they're just crowns that have gone out of style and nobody knew what else to do with them," Hype suggested.

Hype rummaged through a bunch of scrolls and then turned to a pile of huge books. She opened one and found it full of beautiful handwriting, along with very meticulous and colorful artwork, a lot of it containing layers of shiny gold.

Illuminated text, it's called. (Fizzbin)

I think I can make out the words in this one. Talks about a man with horns. That's what the picture shows, too. (Hype)

The OpBot sped over beside Hype's head and began to scan in the text.

That is the Horned Man, to be specific. An old nature deity from ancient England. There are scattered groups of humans who still follow the cult of the Horned Man during this time, but it is a fringe movement. I'll run this against texts we have in the history banks. (Fizzbin)

"Check this out, Hype," Dawk said.

Hype closed the book and walked over to her brother. He was sitting next to an opened wooden chest.

"I found some crazy stuff," Dawk said. "Mummified fingers. Locks of hair. Things that look like pieces of skin. Pretty oogly. Plus a fancy map showing where these were all found. Some place called Creswell Crags. Oh, and this, too."

Dawk held something out to her. Beneath a layer of filth, as if it had been buried for ages, was something white with a slight gleam.

With a shock, Hype realized what it was. She looked closer at the words on the plastic handle: Chicken Flicker.

"A spork?" she whispered. "Like the one we found in Neanderthal times."

That can't be here! We've got to get it out of here! (Hype)

The Faradays knew, from a previous adventure, that the spork was a product of the twentieth century. It definitely did not belong in prehistoric ages, when they first encountered one. And it did not belong in old England either. Someone had pulled it out of the time stream, the continuous flow of events that contained all of history in the proper order, and had stuck it here in a thirteenth-century castle.

The mysterious time traveler again? (Hype)

We'll just steal it. Who would miss it? (Dawk)

Proper procedure calls for the arrangement of a temporal team assigned to remove it. There would be preparations. It requires a lot more planning to remove a spork from a box than you'd think. (Fizzbin)

We should tell Benton about it right away. (Hype)

I have scanned the history banks and can still find no mention of a spork at the wrong point in time. (Fizzbin)

So? (Dawk)

So though this spork might be a temporal irritation to you, it is not a historical disaster. It is not worth making an official report. You are capable of handling it. (Fizzbin)

Aren't you supposed to be keeping us out of trouble? (Hype)

I am doing my best to keep everyone and everything out of trouble, and both my risk and efficiency analyses say this is the smoothest way to do that. (Fizzbin)

Again, what does all that mean? (Dawk)

It means we do nothing right now. We leave the spork where you found it. History will not change before your parents are finished with their mission. We can think about the proper course of action during that time span, and once we decide what to do, we can alert Benton as necessary. (Fizzbin)

Hype placed the spork back in the wooden chest. "Let's get out of here," she said.

"Agreed," Dawk said. "I don't want to run into anything else from the past."

"Or any*one*," added Hype.

CHAPTER

5

The next morning, Dawk and Hype trudged through the mud to Diva's workshop. The village of Nottingham was busy with merchants and shoppers.

Is there anything we can do to help Diva? (Hype)

You heard what your mother said. Tread carefully. (Fizzbin)

You don't have your own ideas about it? You usually do. (Dawk)

I have ideas about temporal issues. Human issues are completely different. I suspect there must be gaps in my programming there. (Fizzbin)

They slogged on until they reached Diva's place, but decided not to knock when they heard angry voices coming from inside.

"Maybe we should come back later," Hype said.

"Can't we just listen in and find out what's going on?" Dawk said.

"This isn't a public battle on the Link, inviting others to jump in," said Hype. This was between two people in the privacy of a home, with the door closed. Sometimes Hype wasn't sure Dawk understood how things really worked in the past eras they visited. She watched her brother creep up to a window and, bending down below it, turn his head upward to listen.

Dawk, that's going too far! (Hype)

What if it's de Babington again? What if he's causing more trouble and she needs to be rescued? (Dawk)

Then we'd better stay out of it. We don't want to attract attention and mess up Mom and Dad's job. And we don't want to end up on another sacrificial altar. (Hype)

Are there any sacrificial altars in Nottingham, Fizzbin? (Dawk)

I need more information before I can answer that. (Fizzbin)

I guess we need to find some hint that there's a time traveler involved before you'll help poor Diva out, huh? When did you get so meek? (Dawk)

Hype sighed. Her brother sure knew how to get under her skin. Hype knew he meant well. It was just that she was trying to stay out of trouble—or, at least, keep her parents from getting in trouble. But she couldn't stand to see people bullied.

All right, tell me if you hear anything. I can bust through the door and spring into action if I have to. (Hype)

Someone gets a little samurai training and suddenly she's a superhero. (Dawk)

If you would like, I can have the OpBot enter and broadcast the conversation to us over the Link. (Fizzbin)

Thank you, Fizzbin. That would be very helpful. (Hype)

Hype saw the OpBot whiz above Dawk's head and through the window. Just as she and her brother had their Visual Cortex Shells programmed to give outsiders a view of them dressed as normal medieval people, the OpBot had its own disguise. No one would see a shining orb from the twenty-fifth century. Instead, its own miniature VC Shell gave viewers the impression of a moth. A fluttering, medieval English moth. Fizzbin prided itself on historical and biological accuracy.

After the moth flew inside the room, Hype began receiving audio through the Link. She could clearly hear Diva and a man who sounded very irritated.

"I can't believe you would support these actions," said the man. "It's disgraceful to both of us."

"He was treated like dirt, and he's giving it back as good as it was handed out to him," Diva answered.

"It certainly puts me in a bad position as the preferred cordwainer of the sheriff," the man said. "I don't know how much longer Nottingham Castle will come to me for their fine footwear while my own father leads a band of rowdies in the forest and robs passing nobles, many of whom are wearing shoes that I made! I wouldn't be surprised if Father has stolen a few pairs."

"You're worried about your own livelihood when your father has been unfairly turned into a fugitive? Roger, you disgust me."

"I am worried about how I will expand my livelihood, to perhaps as far as the King himself. A livelihood that gives you food and a pillow and a roof above your ungrateful head!"

That must be Diva's brother. (Hype)

He sounds really annoying. (Dawk)

"If you are worried about our father, then I would advise you to help de Hedon with his queries about our father's whereabouts," the man said. "I suspect you know more than you say about his hideout. The sooner you help deliver Father to the safety of the law, the sooner this ordeal will be over for our entire family."

"Snooping around, are you?" came another familiar voice. But it wasn't over the Link. Just at that moment, Hype saw a hand grab Dawk's hair. And then it snatched a handful of hers, too.

CHAPTER 6

It was de Babington. "I'm here to collect that friendship tax," he said with a snicker.

Dawk tried to whack de Babington's hand to force him to let go. It worked, sort of. De Babington only let Dawk go after shoving him into the mud.

Hype's mind went through every samurai move she knew, but none of them seemed likely to free her from the under-sheriff's tight grip. Her best bet, she decided, was to remain still and wait until she saw a moment to trip him.

Dawk tried to get up, but de Babington grabbed

him by the arm and started dragging both Faraday siblings through the mud. He hauled them to the front door, which he then kicked open.

"I caught these rodents scurrying outside," he said. "Spying on you. Should I throw them in the dungeon with the rest of the vermin?"

He shoved them both forward onto the rough floor. Dawk and Hype landed in front of Diva and her brother.

"No, thank you, de Babington," Diva said. "These are my friends. I was expecting them just now. So you may go on your way."

"Though my sister is obliged to you for offering your protection," Diva's brother added.

Diva gave him a disgusted look.

De Babington made a swift bow. "I'll see you at the castle soon enough, Roger Godberd, with your foot fineries. And you, good lady . . . I imagine we will blunder into each other over some tax matter or the other."

De Babington winked evilly and then left. Diva ran to Dawk and Hype and helped them up. Dawk was completely covered in mud.

"Friends, are they?" Diva's brother sneered. "Filthy friends, I'd say."

Hype smiled at him. "My name is Hypatia Faraday, and my parents—"

"I don't care who you are," Roger said. "I can see that de Babington seems to know you and that he doesn't like you very much. Now you'll excuse my sister and me, and just slither back to wherever you came from."

Diva slammed her fist down on a nearby workbench. "Enough, brother!" she yelled. "You've stirred things up enough for one day! Go worry about your fancy shoes, and leave me to my trade and my friends!"

"I will leave you," Roger said with a sniff. "If you approve of our father lurking in the dark woods, breathing rebellion, and cavorting with scum, then I'll leave you to your vile companions. Dangerous companions, I should say." Then he stomped off.

"What a charmer," Hype said.

"My brother, my burden," Diva said. "Forgive my rudeness. I should have offered you some fresh water."

"Don't worry about that," Hype said. "Why is your brother so angry with you?"

"He thinks that my father and I are going to ruin his business dealings with the nobles of Nottingham," Diva explained. "He is a high quality cordwainer, and he regularly gets large orders from the sheriff, who likes to show off to the villagers with the fancy boots my brother crafts for him. Roger says that I know where my father is and that I am holding back the truth just to ruin him."

"And do you know where your father is?" asked Dawk.

"Of course I do," Diva said, in a lower voice. "But I'm not keeping it secret to ruin Roger's livelihood. I'm doing it to save my father's neck. He was forced into hiding, and it is because he is a man of honor. He still tries to help the villagers who are pushed around by de Hedon and de Babington."

"What about Grey?" Hype asked. "If those two are bullies, surely Grey can do something about it."

"Grey doesn't control de Hedon," Diva said. "He has a high position at the castle, but he doesn't have any official right to stop de Hedon from being a monster. Since his job hands him every luxury, I expect he wouldn't want to get in any trouble with the king by trying to curb de Hedon's horrible work."

"You said that your father was forced into this life," Dawk said. "How was he forced?"

"Harassed after his allegiance to de Montfort, of course. Now that Henry has control, no friend of de Montfort is safe."

You told us about this de Montfort guy before, Fizzbin. He must have been pretty scary to the people in charge. (Dawk)

Expanding on my earlier information, Simon de Montfort was the sixth Earl of Leicester who rebelled against King Henry III in a scuffle known as the Second Barons' War. (Fizzbin)

So Diva's dad fought in a rebellion? (Hype)

And his side won. It seems de Montfort ran this country after stripping the king of his authority and allowing ordinary citizens to be in charge. Unfortunately, he didn't even last a year. Henry III, the current king of England, defeated him in battle and now hunts down those who are left of de Montfort's followers. (Fizzbin)

So Diva's dad fought in a rebellion that tried to give power to the common person? That's pretty Robin Hood of him. (Dawk)

"It sounds like a horrible situation," Hype told Diva.

"Is there any way we could meet your father?" Dawk asked.

Dawk! (Hype)

What? He sounds amazing! And he might be Robin Hood! (Dawk)

"That could put you in danger," Diva said.

"Danger is practically a hobby for us," Dawk said.

Now who's sounding like a superhero? (Hype)

"We don't want to get you in trouble, either," Hype said. "I know it's not as easy as Dawk thinks it is."

"Well, it's certainly not hard," Diva said. "Since de Hedon and de Babington won't actually go into the woods at night, there's never anyone following me."

"But why don't they go there at night?" asked Hype with a noticeable gulp.

"Oh, they're worried about other dangers," Diva replied.

"Other dangers?" asked Dawk.

"I've not seen nor heard any trace of a black dog, nor Jenny Greentooth, nor even hobgoblins, despite all the terrors Robert of Shepesheved claims are behind every tree," said Diva.

What is she talking about? (Dawk)

No clue. (Hype)

That was a list of terrifying but mythical creatures that lurk in the forest. A ghost dog. A murderous river hag. I don't know what a Robert of Shepesheved is, however. (Fizzbin)

"Who's Robert of Shepesheved?" asked Hype.

"You'll meet him tonight, unfortunately," Diva said. "That is, if you are brave enough to risk the terrors that lurk in the dark of the forest."

"We can do that!" said Dawk.

"When the moon is directly overhead, I'll be at the forest's edge, west of Nottingham, next to the merchant road," Diva told them. "We will have to be careful, and we can't be seen by anyone. If we are caught, we can get arrested, maybe even hanged, because we are trespassing on the King's land. So don't go into the forest without me."

"No problem there," said Hype.

CHAPTER

7

"And you'll have the OpBot with you?" their mother asked. "You're not doing this without an OpBot."

"Don't worry, Mom," Dawk said. "The OpBot will be with us, and we'll be safe."

"Oh, I'm not worried about your safety," Mom said. "I just want to make sure there's a visual record of outlaw footwear. It's a very unique opportunity to add to our current study."

"I wonder if they wear cuffed boots like traditional highwaymen," Dad said, "or whether they had to settle for whatever they had on when they crossed over from citizen to outlaw."

"Or leggings," countered Mom.

"Badger fur linings?"

"Deerskin cutaways?"

"And heels!" said Dad. "I wonder if they've evolved into actual heels?"

"I heard the forest is full of heels," Dawk said.

"Funny," replied Dad. "Funny boy."

I think they're starting to enjoy this shoe study work a bit too much. (Hype)

As long as they're letting us go out into the night and meet Robin Hood, I don't care if we have to take pictures of hats, too. (Dawk)

I don't want to alarm you, but Roger Godberd is just one man alleged to be the inspiration for Robin Hood. (Fizzbin)

Who else is there? (Dawk)

There's Willikin of the Weald, who operated around this same territory about fifty years before your current temporal location. There is Fulk Fitzwarin, who lived west of here around seventy-five years ago. And, of course, Eustace the Monk, around the same time. (Fizzbin)

You can believe in Willikers or Fitzwilly or whoever as much as you want. I know that we are about to meet the real, true Robin Hood. (Dawk)

You've gotten us off track from the actual thing we're supposed to be concentrating on. The spork! What do we do about the spork? (Hype)

Sometimes you need to step away from a problem in order to solve it. (Dawk)

⊙◎ ❖ ◎⊙

Fizzbin dispatched the OpBot to keep watch outside, so when the moon was almost directly overhead, Dawk and Hype got an alert that it was time to go.

The OpBot met them at the castle gate and silently guided them into the chilly night toward the merchant road at the edge of the forest, where Diva would be waiting for them. The quiet was punctuated by squishes of feet in the ever-present mud.

I'm only going so I can keep you out of trouble. (Hype)

Of course. I wouldn't expect you to be interested in meeting Robin Hood at all. (Dawk)

It's not Robin Hood. It's just some outlaw. (Hype)

I'm going to challenge him to an archery contest. (Dawk)

You don't know how to use a bow and arrow. (Hype)

I've done it in PlayMods. What's the difference? (Dawk)

The OpBot light blinked out.

You will be there shortly. (Fizzbin)

Hype squinted into the darkness, as if that would help her see better. It did not, so she kept moving forward in the same direction, hoping that she would soon find Diva.

Then they heard a low cough.

"Diva?" Hype called, grabbing Dawk's hand and dragging him in the direction of the noise.

"You made it," Diva whispered. "And you're sure no one followed you?"

"We were in the clear," Dawk said.

"Then come along and follow me," Diva said. "One of you take my hand, and then take the other's hand, so we don't lose each other. The forest is not very treacherous, but it can seem so in the night."

Hype took Diva's hand and then grabbed Dawk's. They walked along at a healthy pace that surprised Hype, who was unable to see farther than the dark shape of Diva's robe. The ground crackled beneath them as they trudged over sticks and leaves and undergrowth.

"How can you find your way without any light?" Hype asked

"I've done it many times before," Diva said. "My inner compass points to my father."

She uses the stars. (Dawk)

How do you know that? (Hype)

How else? We should learn to do that. (Dawk)

I can have the information transferred into your NeuroCaches for you to access. (Fizzbin)

If I have one more fact transferred into my brain's NeuroCache, I'll have to make room by forgetting how to play a PlayMod. I think I'll pass. (Dawk)

It would be helpful should you need to make a quick escape tonight. (Fizzbin)

Why would we need to make a quick escape? (Hype)

Statistically, it's not unlikely. (Fizzbin)

Hype knew Fizzbin was right. They weren't looking for trouble, but trouble could appear almost anywhere. And, after all, they were headed toward an outlaw hideout.

Diva paused.

Silence.

Then a crack. Rustling.

Hype could have sworn she saw what appeared to be two small, illuminated orbs moving together, then disappearing.

She thought she heard trampling noises following them. Then Diva pulled on Hype's hand and they began moving again.

Hype wasn't sure how long they had been walking when she spied a small burst of orange in the distance. A fire.

"Is that it?" she asked.

"That's it," Diva confirmed.

As the three got closer, Hype could make out figures around the fire and hear murmurs just below the fire's crackling. One of the figures shot up and raised something to his shoulder.

"And who do we have on such a delightful, starry eve?" came a voice.

"I," Diva said. "And two friends."

"And we're sure that these are friends, are we?"

"We're sure."

When Diva led Dawk and Hype closer, Hype could see a man holding a crossbow aimed at them. He was enormous in height and weight, a solid presence.

"Then you may enjoy the warming prickles of our campfire," he said, motioning for them to come forward.

"These are my friends, Dawk and Hype," Diva said as they approached the man.

"It's so good to meet you, Mr. Godberd," Hype said. "Diva has told us—"

"Godberd?" repeated the man. "You mistake me for that no-good varlet Godberd? I'm Devyas, Walter Devyas. You know what we do to friends of Godberd here?"

Is this a trap? (Hype)

I can have Benton pinpoint you and pull you out through the time stream. (Fizzbin)

That guy's big, but I figure if I kick him in the shins, we can make a run for it. (Dawk)

Wait a second. (Hype)

"No," said Hype. "Uh, what do you do to friends of Godberd?"

The man smiled intensely. "We offer them mead and venison, of course!" he said, and he roared with laughter. The other men around the fire laughed, too.

"Enough with your funny business, Devyas," said a shorter, stocky man with a beard and scraggly hair. He walked over to Diva, and she dove into his arms.

"Father," she said.

So that was Roger Godberd. Hype had expected the man behind the Robin Hood myth to be muscular, dashing, and spotlessly clean. But he wasn't that at all.

He looked unkempt—not surprising for someone who had been sleeping in a forest for months on end—and he wasn't good-looking at all. His cheeks were ruddy and had fading scars, and his hair was thinning on top. His nose was large, his eyes were squinty, and his ears stuck out like butterfly wings.

That is definitely not Robin Hood. Where's his hat? (Dawk)

———

CHAPTER

8

Once they took a seat by the campfire, Devyas gave them plates of venison to eat. "But this deer belongs to the king," he warned. "If we're caught eating it, I can't guarantee what good Henry will do about it. Might be off with your heads." He chuckled.

Godberd waved his hand in the air. "These folk aren't used to our rough humor, Devyas," he said. Then he turned to Dawk and Hype and said, "You'll forgive him; he doesn't know how to act around proper guests."

Another voice came from the far side of the fire. "And while it is indeed venison from the king's deer, it was caught fair and square, and with permission." It was another rough-looking fellow, with short gray hair and a mustache, but who looked like he came from civilization instead of the wrong side of the law.

"May I introduce Sir Richard Foliot of Fenwick, our good friend and sometimes benefactor," Godberd said. "He hunted the deer by special permission. He is gracious enough to share it with his disreputable friends."

"My disreputable friends are the most just men in England," Foliot said. "I can't join them in their campaigns, but I can do this for them, and give them occasional shelter at Fenwick."

A young man joined the crowd. He wasn't much older than Hype and had a full beard and scraggly long hair. He smiled and revealed more than one missing tooth.

"Anything causing you shivers tonight?" he asked Diva.

"Something with piercing, yellow eyes lurked

in the darkness," said Diva, "but it seemed not so interested in our kind of flesh."

"This high?" asked the young man, holding his hand to shoulder height.

"I think so," said Hype.

"Black dog," the man said. He held up his left hand, and Hype noticed he was missing a middle finger. "Don't want to mess with them," he added. "They got fierce chompers even though they're ghosts. Fangs that'll pierce your skin and crunch your bones!"

"This is Robert of Shepesheved," said Godberd. "Another of our band."

I knew I saw something. (Hype)

He's making it up, trying to scare us. (Dawk)

He's missing a finger! (Hype)

So? He's missing some teeth, too! (Dawk)

Dawk is correct, Hype. A missing finger is not proof that it was taken by a giant ghost dog. It could easily have been an accident of some sort. (Fizzbin)

"Do you know a lot about the things that go on in this forest?" asked Dawk.

"I know some," Robert said. "This is the land of

Herne, the body of the Green Man, this forest. The soul of the Horned Man. It's a living thing."

"Here he goes with his magical druid ponderings," Devyas said, laughing.

"Enough of you, Devyas," Robert said. "My father and grandfather taught me how the world works and the world beyond. It's more than you see in places like Nottingham, where mortal men dwell. Ancient life hides in the forest, quiet, waiting to return."

"You'll have to forgive Robert," Godberd said. "His family never quite embraced the modern thinking."

"So you believe in the Horned Man?" asked Hype.

She remembered the strange book with the weird illustrations that she and Dawk had discovered in the castle archives.

"Of course I do," Robert said. "My father says the Horned Man was cast out by Æthelberht of Kent along with some of the cunning folk who served him, back when the invaders brought their ways to our island. His spirit lurks here for certain, but one fabled day, his person shall return in bodily form. Men and women will live in peace with the forests once again."

Such honest belief in the Horned Man at this point in English history is very rare. This Robert of Shepesheved is unusual. (Fizzbin)

His smell is unusual, that's for sure. Forest living is leaving a mark on him. (Dawk)

I believe that more pungent aroma is badger mixed with hedgehog. He has uncommon bedfellows. (Fizzbin)

"Enough of this mystical chatter!" Devyas said, laughing. "I say sport! An archery contest, perhaps?" He stood up and gestured Godberd away from the fire.

"You scag, you know I'm no good at archery!" Godberd said. "And I'm worse at it in the dark!"

"Perhaps you'll match me staff for staff?" Devyas asked. "Merely for the amusement of our new friends."

Devyas grabbed a wooden pole from the ground and tossed it over to Godberd, and then he stood holding his own.

"My father is not so bad with a staff," Diva

whispered to Dawk and Hype, "but no one is better than Walter Devyas, I'm afraid."

The two men walked to the edge of the firelight. They each took their place on either end of a huge fallen log. They faced each other, staffs down.

"The object of the sport is to knock your opponent off the log," Diva said. "Devyas will prove the better tonight, as he does every night."

Devyas was the first to make a move. He swung his staff at Godberd's knees in a quick attempt to get him off kilter. As if expecting that move first, Godberd shifted his staff so that it guided Devyas's back up in the air. When Devyas circled his staff back to strike, Godberd held his staff up in a defensive stance and stopped it. The two fighters stood frozen like that for a moment, then Devyas shoved his staff downward with all his might.

The bigger man's weapon slid swiftly between Godberd and his own staff. Devyas yanked both staffs backward, sending Godberd toppling off the log, face-first into the dirt.

Devyas turned toward his spectators and bowed. The outlaws whistled and clapped at the victory.

Godberd pulled himself up from the ground, and Diva dashed across the grass to help him up.

"I shouldn't have taken that challenge," Godberd said.

"Who's next?" cried Devyas. "Any man foolish enough to think he can best me?"

"No man," Hype called out, her hand going up. "But I do!"

What do you think you're doing? (Dawk)

It might be fun. (Hype)

You're going to get clobbered! (Dawk)

I studied naginata with Komatsuhime in Japan, remember? A staff isn't much different. (Hype)

But this is a staff with a monster of a man holding it! (Dawk)

In reference to our earlier conversation, a map of the current sky has been transferred to your NeuroCache. You can use it to read the stars for directions when you are forced to flee this scene. (Fizzbin)

You'd think one of you would have some confidence in me. (Hype)

Hype stood up, handed her plate to Dawk, and began walking toward the log.

"But you're a wee girl," said Devyas.

"Are you afraid of a wee girl?" asked Hype.

"I'm afraid of hurting a wee girl," Devyas told her.

"The wee girl isn't afraid of hurting you," Hype said. The crowd of outlaws cheered.

Diva came over, carrying her father's staff. "You're a strange one," she said as she handed it to Hype. "Aim for his head. It's his softest point."

"I heard that!" roared Devyas.

Do you mind if I finish your venison? I feel like I need to build up my strength for our upcoming escape. (Dawk)

I can't hear you. (Hype)

"A wager!" called Godberd. "If the lass wins, we shall grant her a wish. If she loses, she must launder our outfits and cook us a full meal. Agreed?"

"Agreed," Hype said, nodding.

Do you have any idea how to clean clothes or cook food? (Dawk)

I'll have the information transferred to your NeuroCache. (Fizzbin)

Hype gripped the staff and stood on the log opposite Devyas. She thought back to

Komatsuhime, her combat instructor in ancient Japan, who had taught her various techniques for winning a battle with the smallest possible amount of bloodshed. Komatsuhime had told Hype to figure out what her opponent was forgetting while he was coming up with his strategy, and to strike with that in mind.

The trick was not to let her opponent know that she was analyzing him. Hype stared straight into Devyas's eyes, not letting him know she was thinking of anything other than the upcoming battle.

So what would Walter Devyas not be thinking about?

Hype had an advantage. She had just watched Devyas fight Godberd. What had he concentrated on?

The staff, of course. It was all about the staff.

Hype knew exactly what to exploit in this match.

"Are you sure you want to go through with this?" Devyas asked.

He didn't give Hype a chance to answer. His staff came swinging around at her. She lowered hers to block it, and Devyas seemed surprised by that. He must have expected her to cower and fall before his staff even hit her.

Devyas swung around and Hype matched his move. Then again, and again.

It looked as if he was going to pull the same trick on her as he had on Godberd, inserting his staff behind hers and pulling back, but Hype was too quick.

She moved his staff upward, then twisted hers to the right, which flung his weapon and arms in the same direction and pulled him off balance. As he moved to recover, Hype did a little dance with her feet. That began to shift the log, giving it a slight rolling motion from side to side. Devyas was having a hard time keeping his balance.

Hype released her staff with one hand and let Devyas loose. She was also having some trouble staying on the log while it rocked harder, but she knew she'd only have to hang on a few moments longer than her opponent.

Whomp!

Devyas went flopping off to one side and down

into the mud. Hype steadied the log with her feet, and then leaped down, transforming a potential tumble into a victory step.

The crowd burst into applause and cheering, led by Diva and Dawk, who were jumping up and down in excitement.

"By my oath, I owe the lady something," Godberd said. "She needs only give voice to her wish."

Hype smiled. "I would like you to break into Nottingham Castle and steal something," she said.

Godberd and Devyas both started laughing. The uproar rippled throughout the outlaw camp. Dawk and Diva laughed, too.

No matter how funny it seemed, though, Hype's expression never changed.

"Wait a minute, guys," Dawk said. "I think she's serious."

CHAPTER

9

That was pretty reckless. And I ought to know, because I'm the king of reckless. (Dawk)

It takes care of the spork problem in a way that keeps the two of us out of the picture. Guess I'm not so meek after all. (Hype)

Once Fizzbin runs a risk analysis for temporal anomalies with this scheme, he's going to shoot it down fast. (Dawk)

You must think me an outdated IntelliBoard, Dawk. I have already done a risk analysis and calculated no problems of any statistical note. I even had several other

IntelliBoards analyze my calculations, and they confirm my conclusions. (Fizzbin)

Hype felt Diva's hand squeeze hers tighter as she guided Hype and her brother back to Nottingham through the night woods.

"This scheme of yours had better not put him right in his enemy's lap," Diva whispered. "I worry it's a folly that will have him risk capture. And then I will need to be angry with you, and I don't want to be."

"Don't worry, Diva," Hype told her. "I have a foolproof plan. You won't be angry with me."

A plan that's easier than one of us just going in and grabbing it? (Dawk)

During a time of recorded history, such as this, it is safer to provide a narrative for the disappearance of such an unusual object. Having it disappear alone from the collection highlights its importance to possible observers and makes an issue of it. But having Godberd and his men take it as part of a larger haul puts it in the middle of a larger story and makes it less important as a singular object when measured against the entire haul. (Fizzbin)

But what if he gets caught? (Dawk)

He won't. We have a foolproof plan. (Hype)

History and odds are on our side. And if Godberd were to be captured, that would mean a small fix. (Fizzbin)

A small fix? (Dawk)

Especially when weighed against the calamitous temporal readjustments that a disappearing spork would cause. (Fizzbin)

I don't like the sound of that. And I couldn't even understand half of it. (Dawk)

Finally, they came to the edge of the forest. But before Dawk and Hype turned to walk back to the castle, Diva hugged Hype.

"I believe you, Hype, and I'll try not to worry, " she said. "I just don't want my father spending any more time in the king's jail. And I want him to keep his pride while he runs from the law. Maybe this will help him keep his chest swelled. He loves to brag."

⊙◎ ❖ ◎⊙

"I think it's a wonderful idea," Mom said. "Very clever."

Her husband nodded. "It gets the job done without one of you having to fly around on a synthetic dragon or anything like that."

"And it corrects a problem that I feel like I created," Hype said. "I owe it to the history of the world to handle this, don't you think?"

"I still don't quite get why it's a good idea," Dawk said.

Dawk, any action in the past has the potential to change history. This is why temporal risk analysis is an important aspect of our work at the Cosmos Institute. Sometimes the smallest things make the biggest changes, while the largest ones make no difference at all. (Fizzbin)

"Besides, Fizzbin hasn't even talked about the secret passage yet," Hype said, smiling.

It's called Mortimer's Hole, or will be in another seventy-two years. Currently, it is known as the tunnel from the garden to the castle. (Fizzbin)

Catchy. (Dawk)

It is not something that is part of common castle knowledge. Shall I give you a CartoMod visual? (Fizzbin)

"Please do," said their dad.

All four Faradays felt a burst of directionals in

each of their NeuroCaches, and then a visualization began. All four of them were virtually together inside a CartoMod of Mortimer's Hole.

I've enabled the sharing mode so that the whole family could enjoy this together. (Fizzbin)

Thank you, Fizzbin. (Dad)

The hole wasn't much to look at. It was just a passage of carved-out dirt and rock, large enough for them to stand up hunched over.

There are stairs ahead that lead to the castle entrance. All that will be required of us is to make sure that door is unlocked, and Godberd's men can pass through it safely. (Fizzbin)

What about the archive? How do they get in there? (Dawk)

It is a short distance from the tunnel to the archive. Benton dispatched an OpBot to scan the keys, which he has reproduced and you will find waiting for you on the table in your lodgings as soon as we leave this CartoMod. (Fizzbin)

Good old Benton. (Dad)

The tunnel faded away from around them, and the Faradays found themselves back in their quarters inside Nottingham Castle. On the table where they had left their bread and cheese now lay a ring of metal keys.

Dawk and Hype spent the next day with Diva, who showed them the process for creating parchment from animal skins. They were both a little unsettled by it.

When they returned to the castle, they were not much in the mood for supper.

I warned you. (Fizzbin)

You didn't warn us enough. (Dawk)

I did everything short of providing you with visuals from NeuroPedia. (Fizzbin)

Those poor goats. (Hype)

When they entered the castle, they saw Sheriff de Hedon lurking around, carrying his favorite silver goblet. He looked over at Dawk and Hype suspiciously.

"I wouldn't fraternize with that girl if I were you," de Hedon called to them.

Dawk and Hype both stopped and looked at him across the large hall.

"What girl?" Hype asked.

"The outlaw's daughter," de Hedon said with a sniff. "My under-sheriff tells me everything. I have eyes everywhere in Nottinghamshire."

"I'm sorry, Sheriff de Hedon," Hype interrupted. "Our parents are expecting us for a meal, and I wouldn't want to worry them by being late."

He smiled at Dawk and Hype like a lion watching its prey. "I'm loathe to get you in any sort of trouble," he said.

The siblings rushed away quickly.

Ick. (Hype)

Worse than making parchment. (Dawk)

That night, Dawk and Hype met Diva again at the edge of Sherwood Forest. This time, the encampment had moved farther away, so the trek through the forest in the thick, black night took even longer than it had the first time. Dawk and

Hype were even more wary of the strange sounds they heard in the darkness.

When the three arrived at the camp, they found Godberd and his friends sitting around a low fire. Godberd jumped up and hugged his daughter.

"I am glad you came as well, my friends," he said to Dawk and Hype. "We're eager to talk over the burglary plans."

Hype handed him a map of the castle, and Godberd took it over to the fire and unrolled it to study.

Devyas was there too. He nodded to the three and offered a jug to Hype, who shook her head.

"Maybe you have something softer on the throat and brain for our friends," Diva said.

Robert of Shepesheved appeared with a water skin and handed it to Hype as she and Dawk sat down near the fire. Hype took a swig of it and passed it to her brother.

"No bumps in the night this time, I trust?" said Robert.

Godberd handed the map to Devyas and looked up at Dawk and Hype. "How did you even know about this tunnel?" he asked. "Newcomers and all, I mean. It never crossed our ears."

"As footwear specialists endorsed by the King, our parents have access to all kinds of special information," Dawk said. "They study the impact of the castle floor on boots, for instance, so they need plenty of maps and charts of the castle."

"There is some question in my mind as to how closely your parents might embrace the constable," Devyas said. "Or the sheriff for that matter."

"We never met the constable or sheriff before our arrival," Hype said. "We're just here to do a specific job as representatives of our country of Alvarium. So don't worry. And Reginald Grey doesn't even know about this map."

"What kind of map would put a secret tunnel on it?" Godberd said.

"A secret tunnel map," Dawk said.

"They wouldn't prefer to keep it from the reach of general knowledge?" Godberd asked. "They would just make secret tunnel maps available to anyone who asked?"

"You can trust these two, Father," Diva said.

"I trust you, my daughter," Godberd said. "And therefore I trust your choice of companions." He turned to look at Dawk and Hype. "But, when someone invites us into the house of the law, we will have questions as to whether it is a trap. That is only smart larceny."

"It's not smart until you have this," Hype said, holding up the key to the archive.

"Hmm, I was just planning on kicking the door down," Devyas said.

"The key will make less noise," Dawk said.

CHAPTER

10

Dawk surveyed the landscape. The sheriff's men were gaining on him. Arrows were flying in the air, and all he could do was cover his back with the shield he had stolen from the guard and run like crazy. A few arrows pierced the shield, but not enough to tickle him, let alone hurt him.

He kept running until he came to the tower, where a rope dangled from the upper window. Dawk swung onto it and began climbing. His ultimate goal was to make it to the chamber above with his loot and use the room for protection as he started shooting his own arrows down at the sheriff's men.

With enough skill—and luck, of course—he'd dwindle the number of foes and be able to slide back down and flee into Sherwood Forest.

Halfway up the tower, his sister appeared.

Haven't you played Robin Hood's Ye Big Heiste long enough? (Hype)

I was bored. (Dawk)

You've literally spent all day on PlayMods. It's time to head out to Sherwood Forest and collect our spoils. (Hype)

But this is the first time I've ever tried the tower defense strategy in this PlayMod. (Dawk)

The day of the heist had promised to be a very long day, and Dawk and Hype had agreed that they should stick close to home for it. They had no way of knowing whether the robbery had gone as they'd hoped. At one point, there had been some extra yelling coming from de Hedon, and they noticed more of his men wandering around the castle, but no news or evidence of the outlaws.

At sundown, Fizzbin sent the OpBot out for

a spin to find out whether it was safe to leave the castle.

They have guards at the archive now, but otherwise it's clear. (Fizzbin)

Maybe we should take the tunnel, just to be safe and make sure there aren't any guards lurking around the outside of the castle. (Dawk)

I think that's a good idea. (Hype)

The real tunnel was squishier than the CartoMod version, and it also stank of worms. But besides that, with the OpBot providing light, it was easy enough for Dawk and Hype to reach the end.

Hype climbed out first. They found themselves in a quiet grove in the castle's deer park, which was part of the larger forest. The OpBot led them to Diva, who was hiding behind a tree. She seemed more excited than they had ever seen her.

"My father took extra with this haul," Diva whispered. "You'll both see. It will take a while."

They all clasped hands and moved deeper into the forest. This walk was longer, and Diva dragged them along at a quicker pace until a familiar flicker of orange appeared in the distance. It appeared to be coming from a cave set into a huge hill or cliff, and they could hear faint singing.

"Inside," Diva whispered.

Near the entrance, a group of horses had been corralled. Their reins were tethered to huge rocks, and each horse's saddlebags were stuffed with the loot from the castle archive.

As Dawk, Hype, and Diva marched into the cave, they found Godberd, Devyas, Robert, and a few more outlaws singing off-key and slinging mugs together.

"Should they be singing that loud?" Dawk asked.

"They're very happy," said Diva.

"The sheriff will be happy, too, if he's searching the forest," Dawk said. "The singing will lead him right here. And it's not very good singing, anyway."

"Nottingham and Sherwood Forest are a maze of caves," Diva said. "The idiot sheriff would have to find this exact one before they even heard the singing, and that would take some time."

"Come, come to the fire!" said Godberd, gesturing to them. "Will you have something to celebrate with?"

Devyas saw them and held a mug in the air. "Ah, girl, I challenge you to a rematch!" he said, laughing.

"Another night, Devyas," Hype told him. "You look too tired to take me on."

"Plucky lass." Devyas grinned.

Robert of Shepesheved wandered over, holding something in his hand. He smiled and revealed his missing teeth. Then he held something out to Hype. "This is for you," he said. "For luck."

He dropped a carved stone into Hype's outspread palm.

"It's the Horned Man!" she exclaimed.

"His spirit will protect you as long as you are in the forest," Robert said. "They also told me I could give you this." From a pouch at his belt, he produced a small white object.

The spork! (Hype, Dawk, and Fizzbin)

Hype grabbed it. "Thank you, Robert," she said. "For both."

"It's a strange object, it is," Robert said. "Whatever is it made from? Is it magic?"

Hype smiled. "I guess it is sort of magical. But probably not in the way you're thinking."

Dawk glanced down at the spork. "At least one thing has gone right," he said.

What are the things that aren't going right? (Hype)

I think we were followed. (Dawk)

What?! Why do you think we were followed? (Hype)

I heard noise outside, like animals. (Dawk)

You're sure it's not a black dog? (Hype)

I sent the OpBot out to scan, and I found that several horses with riders were scanned in the vicinity. I would also like to point out that ghostly black dogs do not exist, which makes it unlikely they are what Dawk spotted. (Fizzbin)

What should we do? (Hype)

Maybe the criminal mastermind will allow me to handle this. (Dawk)

"Attention, everyone!" Dawk called.

Should you yell like that? (Hype)

No worse than their singing. (Dawk)

"I need to know something, and I need to know it now," Dawk said. "Is there a back way out of this cave?"

"There is only the entrance you came through," Godberd said. "Why?"

"Because the sheriff and his men are gathering outside the cave," Dawk said.

"How do you know this?" asked Devyas, rushing toward the cave entrance to peer out. "This is an unmapped cave. No one knows it's here except us."

"We have two choices," Godberd said. "We can sit around the cave and discuss the matter, or we can make a run for it. I'd suggest my daughter and our guests hop rides with the three of us—Devyas, Robert, and me. The other men should spread in all directions. The sheriff will be pulled all ways, and fewer of his men will follow us. We'll meet at Creswell Crags."

Godberd gave his remaining men their directions for the night and then rushed to the horses. He mounted his horse, and Diva joined him.

"If we can lose them in the night, the Crags will provide shelter during the day," Godberd told them all. "It's a long enough ride that the sheriff might give up before he gets there. We regroup north side of the pond, fourth cave going east. There will be plenty of room to house the horses and ourselves."

I suggest you hurry. (Fizzbin)

"The key," Godberd said, "is to burst out of here in a fury, before they realize we are doing so. I will next see you all when sun has risen."

What do we do now? (Hype)

Climb on a horse and hold on for your life! (Dawk)

CHAPTER

11

Hype clung tightly to Robert of Shepesheved's waist as his horse sped through the night. She couldn't see anything in the darkness, but leaves and small branches whacked her head and shoulders.

How do these horses not bump into trees? I can't see a thing! (Hype)

I'd definitely need some kind of special goggles, or maybe a retina modification. (Dawk)

It was hard to tell where the sheriff and his men were, since the pounding of the horses' hooves drowned everything else out.

Fizzbin, what is Creswell Crags, anyhow? (Hype)

The history banks indicate it to be a series of interconnected limestone caves that have been in use, on and off, for thousands of years. A sound hiding place, it seems. (Fizzbin)

And a faraway one. (Hype)

Time passed slowly on the back of a horse in a mad dash from the law. Dawk and Hype were relieved when someone yelled that the Crags were ahead. The horses slowed down as they moved past a body of water glimmering in the moonlight. Then Hype could hear Robert's voice counting quietly.

"Keep your head low," Robert whispered.

Then it seemed as if his horse dashed straight into a wall.

The change was obvious right away. The horses' hooves clomped on a harder surface, and the darkness was more complete.

We're definitely in a cave now. (Dawk)

The horses stopped, and the riders dismounted.

"We're here for the night, maybe longer," Godberd said. "I suggest we each find a soft portion of rock for a pillow and catch as much sleep as we can. Tomorrow will demand all of our strength. I'll take watch first. Then Devyas."

Dawk and Hype fumbled around in the dark, their arms flailing, trying to find the sides of the cave. Hype grabbed Dawk's arm and dragged him to one side, and then down onto the ground.

We have to sleep in here? (Dawk)

No, but we do have to sit here in the dark and be quiet for hours after a rough horse ride where everything hurts. If sleep will make things move along faster, that's an option. (Hype)

Both of them lay on the floor of the cave, side by side, hoping nothing too disgusting was crawling around them. All Hype could think of were phantom dogs and druids and witches. She gripped the stone Robert had given her. Even though she couldn't see it in the darkness of the cave, the image of the Horned Man gave her a sense of comfort. Soon she heard Dawk snoring next to her. And then, slowly, she drifted off to sleep.

Dim light greeted Dawk when he opened his eyes. Sunlight was peeping into the caves from somewhere unseen. Hype was already on the other side of the cave, pointing at something and whispering to Diva, while the three outlaws stood silently together at the entrance, keeping an eye and ear out for the sheriff.

Dawk stood up and stretched his aching body. Cave floors were worse than the worst medieval bed.

This cave isn't as gross as I thought it would look. (Dawk)

I believe I have something that humans would find funny. Geographic cross-referencing within the history banks, and also a few CartoMods capturing this area in the twentieth century, reveal to me that the very cave you are in was, at one time, referred to as Robin Hood Cave. Are you laughing as a result of me telling you that? (Fizzbin)

No. (Dawk)

"Good morning, sir!" Diva said, smiling at Dawk. "Come here and look at these pretties we found."

She pointed at the cave wall next to where she and Hype were standing. Dawk leaned closer. The wall was covered with carvings. Typical caveman stuff—hunting, the sky, the forest, other cavemen. Neanderthals, by the look of it.

Neat. Looks like the Neanderthals who lived here were telling some kind of history of themselves. Fizzbin, have you had the OpBot scan this? (Dawk)

Those carvings are already in the history banks, so there is no point. (Fizzbin)

Dawk continued along the path of images and came to a sudden stop, running his fingers slowly over something on the rocky surface.

Do the history banks show what I'm seeing? You might want to get the OpBot over here. You, too, Hype. (Dawk)

The OpBot, disguised as a moth, fluttered over and began hovering around the carvings, with Hype slowly creeping up to take a look.

Tell me what you think, because I think this place looks pretty familiar. (Dawk)

While Hype leaned in closer to the carvings, Dawk got up and walked to the cave entrance.

"No sign of our pursuers," Godberd told him. "I trust you were able to get some sleep."

"Rocks make horrible pillows," Dawk said. "Is it safe for me to peek out?"

Godberd nodded, and Dawk moved closer to the cave's entrance. He looked out and scanned the area.

We've been here before. Not in a very long time by Earth chronology, but we have been here. (Dawk)

Yeah, and I think these carvings prove that. (Hype)

Dawk turned around. Hype was still looking closely at the carvings.

You see what I saw? (Dawk)

I see four figures that don't look like the others disappearing into the air. And then I see two of those figures appearing out of the sky and giving one of the figures a small white object. (Hype)

The spork! (Dawk)

That cave drawing documents your previous interactions with the Neanderthals. But at some point in the future, you need to go back to a point before your first visit and give the very spork you have been carrying to the Neanderthals. (Fizzbin)

What if we don't? How would that affect the past? (Dawk)

The time stream exists as the time stream exists. We don't know whether your actions changed it or maintained it. I believe the best solution is the simplest one in this case—do what history dictates, close the circle, and move on to more important temporal matters. (Fizzbin)

And then afterward, maybe we can chart the history of that spork, just for fun. (Dawk)

"But it would get the horses refreshed, and we could safely be on our way," came Devyas's stern voice. Dawk wandered closer to hear more.

"We have no clue whether the sheriff lies in wait," Godberd said. "If we take the horses out to water and they descend on us, it's over. That could be why none of the other men have shown up— they were captured."

"One of us could go out," Robert said. "I'm not afraid of the sheriff."

"Thank you, Robert, but we need you with us more than we need you with the sheriff," Godberd said.

"I'll go," Dawk said. "Not with a horse. Just me. I'm smaller than any of you, so I can scout the area and report back."

"What if you don't report back?" asked Devyas.

"Then you know," Dawk said.

Is this a smart idea? (Hype)

The smartest. I go out, do some token crawling around and scouting, but Fizzbin will send the OpBot out and do a massive sweep to let us know exactly what's going on. If it sees the sheriff or anybody, we'll know, and I can come back and say I saw it. (Dawk)

I would say it is currently your best bet. (Fizzbin)

"All right, boy," Godberd said, patting Dawk on the shoulder. "Off with you then. At a certain point, if you don't return, we'll assume the worst and flee the caves."

"I'll be back," Dawk assured him. "I'm not going to be captured by the sheriff. That guy is a jerk."

Dawk stepped out of the cave and slinked along the side of the cliff, stooping down until he was out of the outlaws' sight. The OpBot, disguised as a dragonfly, darted along the nearby water and deeper into the woods.

Robert noticed Hype opening and closing her hand over her stone of the Horned Man. "I'm glad you are happy with your treasure," he said.

"Yes, thank you. And what about you?" asked Hype. "What treasures did you find for yourself?"

Robert grabbed one of his saddlebags and excitedly opened it up. "Not the sorts of treasures that would bring you money," he said. "The sorts of treasures that bring you dreams."

He began feeling around in the bag and pulled something out. "Like this!" he said, laughing.

It was a stiff, withered, pointy human finger.

"I have my ideas who this belonged to," he said, "but I don't want to say until I'm sure of it. There are other strange things as well."

"Robert's eyes don't always go to the gold," Devyas called over. "Too smart for a thief. He would make a fine husband to some lady, if not for being wanted by the law."

Robert smiled his mostly toothless smile. "Ah,

I forgot the strangest one yet," he said, rooting around in his bag.

He pulled out something and presented it open-palmed to Hype.

Fizzbin, I'm looking at a portable time gadget from our future, like the one we found in Prague. Robert of Shepesheved took it as part of his haul from the archive. (Hype)

Do you think he would part with it easily? (Fizzbin)

I'll try to find out. (Hype)

There was a scuttling at the cave entrance, and Hype turned quickly to see what was going on. Diva was helping Dawk to his feet. He was out of breath.

"What did you see, boy?" asked Godberd.

"I don't know how many of them there are exactly," Dawk said, "but hundreds would be a safe guess."

There are exactly 374, not including the servants who have accompanied the various members of this small army of lawmen. (Fizzbin)

Yeah, and thanks to the OpBot, I see that one of them is Diva's brother, Roger Godberd Jr., so we know how they found the outlaw hideout. I'll bet he's been following Diva for days to find his father. (Dawk)

I didn't think he would betray his dad and sister. (Hype)

"Hundreds?" Godberd said. "Pursuing us?"

"I told you that you were a bigger pain in their posteriors than you gave yourself credit for," Devyas said.

"Where do these caves lead?" Dawk asked.

"They go in farther," Devyas said, "but they eventually come to an end."

"I don't see any way out of this," Godberd said. "Flee, fight, surrender."

"What will happen if you're caught?" Hype said.

"We'll all be hanged," Devyas said. "You as well. And probably your father and mother, too, as co-conspirators."

I can have Benton pull you from this cave. (Fizzbin)

But what about our friends? (Hype)

I don't believe he would pick them up. (Fizzbin)

We can't leave them to be hanged! (Hype)

"I know a way out," Hype said. "But you're going to have to trust me."

"We've trusted you so far, and look where it's gotten us," Devyas said.

"Oh, leave her alone," said Robert. "She didn't do anything."

"What is your plan?" Diva asked.

"Robert, can I borrow your strangest treasure?" Hype asked.

"Take it if it provides you some comfort in this situation," he said, handing the time gadget to her.

Where did he get that? (Dawk)

I'll explain later. (Hype)

Aloud, Hype said, "Right now, I need everyone to put their hands on each other's shoulders so that we are all connected physically."

Everyone did as they were told. Hype put her finger on the gadget, which made an electronic beep, followed by a green light.

Fizzbin, we're going to be out of touch for a while. Wherever we're going, I doubt there's going to be a LinkStream from the twenty-fifth century to follow us. Stand by till we reappear. (Hype)

What are you planning, Hype? (Fizzbin)

"I need everyone to take a deep breath," Hype said.

She moved her finger along the top casing of the gadget. The green light turned to yellow. There was a sudden burst of energy around the six of them, and they disappeared.

CHAPTER

12

Wherever—or whenever—they were, it sort of looked like the twenty-fifth century, just a little more run-down, with enclosed corridors and scuffed black floors, no personality to distinguish it as special. It looked a lot like the Alvarium, but the silence in their heads alerted both Dawk and Hype that there was no LinkStream available, and so there was no Fizzbin to give them a smart answer about where they were exactly.

The last time Dawk and Hype had used one of the time gadgets from their future, during a mad dash through time in Prague, it hadn't transported them through space. Just time.

But now, instead of finding themselves in the cave in a different era, they were somewhere else entirely.

The outlaws and Diva looked stunned.

"Where are we?" Godberd asked. "And how did we get here?"

"I know how we got here," Dawk muttered, "but I have no clue where we are."

"I have never seen walls so smooth," Devyas said. "Or bright. What manner of stone is this?"

"It's wood," said Robert. "Don't you know wood when you see it? You can't get rock like that."

"And what do you know of it?" Devyas asked. "No longer just a thief, I see, now you're some kind of builder?"

"Keep it down until Hype figures out where we are," Diva snapped.

Hype and Dawk walked along the corridor and found that it soon led to another corridor.

"When we find our way back to Mom and Dad, can I blame you for this?" asked Dawk.

"Wouldn't you anyway?" replied Hype.

"If I didn't know any better, I would say we're in the Alvarium," Dawk said.

"I feel pretty sure we're in the Alvarium. Just not our Alvarium," Hype said.

The corridor continued for a hundred feet or so before ending in a larger space.

"If that's the Mall at the end of this, I'd say it's our Alvarium," Dawk said.

"Our Alvarium, maybe. Just not *when* we knew it," Hype said. More loudly, she called, "Come on. Follow us."

They walked down the hallway as a group. Sure enough, they soon arrived at the public center of the Alvarium, the Mall. It was a huge open area surrounded by towering walkways, and it was completely abandoned.

"This is a magnificent palace," said Godberd. "I wonder who it belongs to."

"That swine King Henry, of course," Devyas said. "Who else?"

"I think it must be a sorcerer's home," said Robert.

"Or heaven," Diva said. "I wouldn't rule out heaven."

"Heaven could use a little cleaning up," Dawk mumbled.

A high-pitched tone filled the air, bouncing around the high walls of the Mall and stopping the conversation. Everyone in the group covered their ears to muffle the noise, and ran back into the corridor. The siren was slightly muffled there.

"If this is heaven, then the gods are angry," Devyas said.

"I still think it's a sorcerer," said Robert.

Dawk grabbed the time device from Hype's hand. "Look, everyone, what Hype did before, I'm going to do now," he said. "Let's all join together again and get out of here."

They did as he asked. Dawk fiddled with the screen, but no matter how he swished his fingers, the green light on it never turned yellow. He began poking it angrily with his index finger, but that didn't do any good either. Suddenly, the green light went out. The gadget seemed dead.

"I think Hype must have broken it," Dawk said.

The awful noise was still blaring. But they also began to hear thuds, and then Dawk saw large, awkward figures scuttling around in the Mall. One of them stopped moving and turned toward the corridor.

The figure was built like a human, but instead of a face, it just had two eyes, and instead of ears, there were just holes. The being wasn't wearing clothes, but it didn't seem naked, either, even though what covered it looked just like skin.

"What is that?" asked Dawk.

"It's a monstrosity on two legs," said Robert. "It can't be human."

"That's a FleshBot," Hype whispered to her brother. "It has to be."

They all ran at the same time, heading the opposite way down the corridor. More creatures like the first spilled in from the Mall, and all of the beings chased after Dawk, Hype, and the outlaws.

"Where are we going?" Hype asked as she ran.

"I don't know yet!" Dawk called back. "I've got some location data in my NeuroCache that might help us."

Dawk's NeuroCache was filled with tons of information that had been placed there for times when he might find himself in trouble and with no access to the Link. Like now. He found a data file called "Alvarium Ground Plans" that was stored in a data cluster tagged "Emergencies," which this was. The file was a complete map of the Alvarium, revealing hundreds of nooks and crannies that Dawk had no clue ever existed.

"There's a door to the right about five hundred meters ahead," Dawk called back to Hype. "It will say 'Curator Corridor to Heritage Vault.' Or at least it did . . . or will at some point. I'm hoping we can get through it."

The door was where the data had predicted, but it didn't open automatically. A sign lit up that read "Neural Bypass Identification Required." Dawk moved his forehead closer to a small sensor under the sign. A red beam of light projected onto his head.

"Identity confirmed. Faraday, Dawkins. Last known assignment: Historical Underwear Research Division. NeuroNet upgrade six hundred years overdue. Enter," read the sign above the door, and the door slid open. The group pushed their way in.

Once they were inside, the door slid closed. It was a spare space, drab gray walls with equally uninteresting seating spaces and old-fashioned data screens covered in dust that didn't look like they had been used for years. The hulking creatures could be heard rampaging past outside.

Dawk leaned over to Hype and whispered, "Alvarium computer banks are telling me I'm six hundred years overdue for a NeuroNet upgrade, so we're definitely in the future. And I'm listed as working in the Historical Underwear Research Division. Is that what I'm going to end up doing with my life? Underwear? What a waste!"

"At least we're safe for now," Hype said. "We are safe, right? Where are we?"

"The Curator Corridor to the Heritage Vault, whatever that is," Dawk said.

"Have you been to this little room in heaven before?" Diva asked.

"No, never," Hype said. "I don't even know what it is."

Dawk paused while he accessed his NeuroCache. Then he pointed farther back in the room.

"If we keep moving, we'll find a passage," he said. "It circles around a huge space in the middle that seems to be a series of separate, but connected, rooms. I think there are doorways from the circular passage into the other place with all the rooms. I don't know what the other place is, but it's out of the way enough from the main corridors that it should keep us safe for now."

Dawk and Hype led the way, ahead of the rest of the group.

"They seem to be taking this well," Dawk whispered.

"Probably because they're coming up with all sorts of supernatural explanations for what they're seeing," Hype whispered back. "Do you have any actual idea where this passage in your head is leading us?"

"I just know it's there," said Dawk. "But I don't know what it is."

At the back of the room was an entrance to a winding, metallic corridor.

As they walked down the hall, they passed pairs of translucent sliding doors. Each set of doors looked into what appeared to be a room in a museum, with display cases and items hanging on the walls. With no odd FleshBots chasing them, Hype and Dawk felt safe stopping to peer through some of the doors.

"Look at all those paintings," Hype marveled as they stared through one door. "I wonder if we could get in there and get a closer look."

She moved her hand along the side of the door. Its edges illuminated, and the door slid open. The group slowly walked into the room, which appeared to be a midsized gallery of some sort, with illuminated glass cases placed in the middle and pictures hanging on the wall all around.

One painting on the wall showed a strange-looking bald man grasping his face and apparently screaming from some kind of terror or despair. Dawk walked up to it and smirked. "Well, that captures how I feel right now," he said.

There were other interesting paintings, too. A huge one of sunflowers and another of a crazy blue sky and giant stars over an old-fashioned town. There were also pictures of humans that didn't look quite like humans—for instance, one was made of colored triangles and had two eyes on one side of its face.

"Picasso," Hype read on a plaque.

"Mutants," Dawk murmured.

Some of the outlaws went back into the corridor, so Dawk and Hype followed them. "Look at this treasure trove, Roger!" Devyas called from the entrance into another room. That room's sign read "Historical Armory."

The room was filled with all sorts of weaponry, from large cannons to small but deadly-looking axes, chains with prickly spikes at the end, and even more sophisticated technology that looked like laser rifles. On the far left side of the room was a display of Japanese weaponry, including a naginata, the weapon Hype had learned to use during their trip to medieval Japan.

"We might want to smash through that glass and grab those," Dawk said. "It might help us if those big weirdos catch up with us."

"Big weirdos?" came an unfamiliar voice.

Dawk turned. A young woman, her arms crossed, stood in the doorway. She had short black hair and wore a black bodysuit and an intense stare.

"So you're the ones the Synthmanoids were after," she said. "We set up the security system to give them a purpose, but I'm afraid they aren't very good at it." The woman smirked at them as if she had just tricked them.

"Where are we?" asked Hype. "And when?"

"You're in the year 3132," the woman said, "in the underbelly of the Alvarium, the forgotten museum of the past. Citizens haven't bothered to visit for a thousand years." The woman grinned. "My name is Curator. I've been looking forward to this day for a long, long time, Dawk and Hype Faraday, but when I woke up this morning I never expected today was the day."

CHAPTER 13

"Do we know you?" Hype asked the mysterious woman.

"We've met," the woman said. "However, I know you better than you know me. I've met you a few times, some of which haven't actually happened for you yet, and some which you don't even know about because I'm a very good actress."

"Antevorta?" asked Hype.

"Curator," the woman said. "My name is Curator."

"Curator or High Priestess or whatever you

want to call yourself," Dawk said, "the last time we met, you had a giant crab monster almost bite my head off. I'm not in the mood to be Mr. Smiley McFriendly with you."

"A giant crab?" asked Curator. "That hasn't happened yet in my timeline. I'd remember it if it had. Good idea, though. Thank you."

"You and Dawk can chatter on later," Diva said, "but right now I want to know about the monsters. Are they yours? Are we safe from them?"

"Oh, you're safe from them, certainly," Curator said. "Those useless beasts aren't mine, no, and they won't come down here to the Heritage Vault. Not allowed. They'd tear apart all this valuable history in their doltish attempt to do their job. Hundreds and hundreds of years of hard work by people like your parents would be destroyed. It would be dreadful, don't you think? All that history down the tubes. It would make my job harder, anyhow."

Curator held out her hand and beckoned the six of them forward. "Please, let me show you around the collection," she said.

"Can I ask you some questions first?" Hype asked. "How do we know you're not leading us into a trap?"

Curator paused for a moment, looking distracted. "You're already in a trap, basically, don't you think?" she said. "But, yes, of course. Why not? Ask your questions. Voice tells me Voice wants you to ask, and Voice overrides me."

"Voice? Who is Voice?" asked Dawk.

"Voice is Voice, that's who," said Curator. "Voice is just there. Voice has always been there, on-Link. My mentor, my guide. A bit like your Fizzbin, but not as irritating."

"You said we've met before. So are you behind all the temporal meddling that we've run into?" asked Hype. "Or is it Voice that's doing it?"

"It is me, it is Voice," said Curator. "I do these things for Voice. To keep Voice amused."

"This one seems a few dings short of a bell," said Devyas. "I say she's a waste of time. We have more important things to attend to. Look around you, Godberd! This armory—it is our ticket to a free country. No one could stand up to this bewitched weaponry. The rebellion will be reborn, and we will triumph with all this behind it."

"That's a thought," said Godberd. "We'd have to learn how some of this works."

"You're going to have to trust us," Hype said. "We can't just stay here and look at weapons. This— what Curator is telling us—is more important than the sheriff or King Henry or whatever else you're dealing with."

"More important?" said Godberd angrily. "We barely know who you are and we do you a favor, which gets us cornered by the sheriff and whisked off to some magical castle. We meet this barmy girl who talks in circles, and you have the nerve to tell us that what we do know from our own lives has no importance?"

He snorted, then continued. "Look around at all this armament. I see what Devyas is leading to. We gather it up, bring it back with us, arm all my men and others, and I see not only an England free of the sheriff and his like, but one in the spirit of my lord, de Montfort, with whom I fought."

"You're not stealing hover tanks and plasma

bazookas and laser guns," Dawk said. "You can't take those with you to fight a revolution. You'd blow the whole time stream apart."

"What stands between us and the weapons?" asked Godberd, smirking. "Children? Children who think they can block a free England, ruled by the English people."

"My, this is an unexpected delight," said Curator. "Neither Voice nor I had any idea our little game would take this turn. It had not registered before in any versions of the universe. Voice says that Voice is very amused. The best game yet! I have to agree with Voice on this one. This is delicious."

"I'd like to speak to Voice," said Hype.

"Oh, Hype, you need to be on our Link to do that, and surely you've realized by now that you can't access our Link," Curator said. "Your neural bypass is too outdated—too limited, you see. You need a BioPass at birth, like everyone else in my time. And there's no temporal stream here for your link, as you've no doubt noticed. Of course, there is the Outmoded Passage, which would provide physical transport for you as in the pre-NeuroNet days. That is, if Voice approves."

"What is she blabbing on about?" asked Godberd. "And what has this got to do with liberating England?"

"She is the sorceress behind this trickery," said Robert. "Her own army of demons hunts us down while we hide in her armory. May Herne the Hunter help us!"

"Well, I don't see what's stopping us from fighting back," said Devyas. He stormed toward a glass case filled with laser guns and smashed it open.

"Voice finds this quite amazing," said Curator. "Such fun!"

Devyas reached into the case, grabbing a laser gun, but the sound of more glass shattering made him stop and turn.

It was Dawk and Hype, kicking through the Japanese weaponry display case. Hype grabbed the naginata and dashed toward Devyas, who stood dumbfounded.

"You know I can beat you at anything, Devyas!" she yelled, waving the naginata at him. Devyas jumped back and dropped the laser gun. "You don't even know how to use that!" she cried.

"Voice is enjoying this!" Curator said, beaming.

"Can I ask a question?" Dawk said. "If Robin Hood and Little John are done trying to steal weapons, I would like to backtrack a little bit. What exactly is the Outmoded Passage?"

"Oh, Voice said that would be delightful," Curator said. "Voice has always wanted to meet you both. You must take the Outmoded Passage and meet Voice."

"I don't know if I want to do that alone," Dawk said.

"What do you mean do it alone?" Hype asked. "Did you forget about me?"

"If you go, who's going to keep Robin Hood from stealing all the weapons?" said Dawk.

Hype glanced around at the outlaws in the room, weighing her options. It didn't look promising.

Curator laughed. "I hadn't even thought of that, but now that you mention it, it sounds like a wonderfully sinister plan! Would you boys like to get your hands on an antimatter tank?"

"Why is her auntie mad?" Devyas asked no one in particular.

"I'll keep them under control," Diva said.

"Diva might have her father wrapped around her finger, but she'll not lord over me!" barked Devyas.

"Nor me!" echoed Robert.

"You two have no choice," smiled Diva, pulling the laser gun that Devyas dropped from behind her back.

She held it up at them and nodded to Hype. "And I'm not afraid of Curator, either," Diva said.

"I guess the two of us have a date with Voice." Dawk smiled at Hype.

"You'll have to follow me," said Curator. "Voice is a few galleries away."

Curator calmly strolled out of the armory. Hype waved her naginata at the medieval outlaws, and they followed, with Diva coming up behind them.

"I never thought I'd see the day my own daughter held arms against me," Godberd said.

"I never thought I'd see the day where I'd feel worse if I didn't," Diva told him.

In front of the outlaws, Hype leaned into Dawk even as she kept an eye on them.

"I'm concerned whether Diva is up to the job, but even if they get weapons, they can't go anywhere with them," she whispered to her brother.

"I'm just afraid that if they get the weapons, this Voice she keeps talking about will help them go somewhere," Dawk whispered. "That would make this go from bad to worse pretty quickly."

"I just hope the laser gun still works," Hype said. "I wish we could ask Fizzbin what their typical shelf life is."

Curator led them through several adjoining rooms, each fairly large and featuring a different theme. Godberd, Devyas, and Robert were gawking at everything, causing Diva to have to push them along to hurry them up.

One room was filled with the tools of alchemy, another with women's fashions through the ages. Still another featured the history of art, including the Neanderthal panels that Dawk, Hype, and Diva had just been looking at in the cave minutes before. It seemed like the complete, intricate history of humanity was in this museum complex under the Alvarium.

"I just thought of something," Dawk whispered to Hype. "When we were in Japan and Fizzbin's backup was in my NeuroCache, he told me something. He said, '3132. You have been there.' I didn't know what that meant at the time."

"He must have seen in the future computer banks that we had visited the year 3132," Hype whispered.

"Otherwise known as now," said Dawk.

"And are you enjoying the Heritage Vault?" Curator asked.

"When was it built?" Hype asked.

"It was built when the Alvarium was built," Curator said. "It was here in the twenty-fifth century, but no one bothered to seek it out. Now, citizens live on-Link and in hyper-immersive vRealities by their own choice. There's no one left, other than me, to even notice this place. Who needs the physical anymore?"

They were in a large room marked "Multiversal Connectivity Engineering," which contained several gray, rounded, pod-like containers that resembled futuristic shower units, but with lights and indicators on the outside.

Curator stopped at one. "This one will take you to Voice," she said. "I'm certain it still functions, though it has not been used in centuries. Hopefully we won't have an accident."

"And Voice is the one who has been tampering with history?" Dawk asked.

"It isn't tampering," Curator said. "It's playing. And give me some credit for my part in this, please."

"Is this some kind of magical cabinet?" Godberd asked. "Strange material."

"Hands off, Father," Diva said.

Dawk smiled at Hype. "I guess we have to do this, huh?" he asked.

"We could just try to get back home and let Benton and the Chancellor handle it," Hype said.

"But when have we ever done that?" Dawk asked.

Curator motioned to the contraption.

"You step inside," Curator said. "I will do the rest out here."

Hype called out to Diva and tossed her naginata to her. Diva caught it, still holding the laser gun firmly.

"You'll keep that for me while I'm gone, right?" asked Hype.

"Not that I understand where you are going," said Diva, "but I'll do it."

"You'll need it in case the laser gun jams," Hype said.

Curator opened a panel, and Dawk and Hype stepped inside.

"Are you sure this isn't a trap?" Dawk asked.

"That would have no place in Voice's game," Curator said, shutting the panel behind them.

Dawk and Hype stood inside the chamber, looking out at Diva and the outlaws with barely an idea of where they were really going or what would happen when they got there. But they also both knew that they were getting closer to understanding the mysteries that had chased them as they tripped along through time.

Everything began to fade away and, as if by instinct, Dawk grabbed Hype's hand, holding tightly until there was nothing else left anywhere but the sight of the two of them.

CHAPTER

14

Dawk could not tell where he was, but he could still feel Hype's hand. He wasn't really sure if he was standing or sitting.

"Hype?" he whispered. "Hype?"

"I'm here," Hype answered. "I don't know where here is, though."

Everything was blank. That's the best way Dawk could figure it. Nothingness, but with little glimmers of somethingness that seemed to be forming into a shape that looked familiar. A garden? A Japanese garden. With a castle wall around it. Dawk and his sister were sitting on the ground. Were they back in Japan?

A figure appeared. Short. A girl. Dawk knew her.

"Hello, Dawk," she said.

It was Junko, his friend from medieval Japan.

"Junko?" Dawk said. "What are you doing here?"

"And do you happen to know where here is?" Hype asked.

"You are here," Junko said.

"Where is here?" Dawk asked.

"Where I am," said Junko.

"Which is . . . ?" Hype asked.

"Does this bodily form not put you at ease?" Junko asked. "I thought it would, but I seem to be wrong. Would you prefer a different form?"

"I don't think you're Junko," Dawk said. "Who are you?"

"I am here," said Junko. "Here is who I am."

"I don't understand," Dawk said.

"Neither of us do," Hype said.

"I don't have a name for myself. Curator calls me Voice. That's the name I answer to most often. You have a name for me, too. You call me the DataVerse.

I am where all the information from your universe is stored, to keep history safe."

"So then where are we?" asked Hype. "Can you give us a straight answer?"

"You are here," said Voice. "You are in me. And at this point of the game, you are here because I am prepared to tell you anything you wish to know. Consider it a cheat, I suppose."

"So you're just taking on Junko's appearance?" Dawk asked. "And we're not in Japan again?"

"No, this is all data that I have translated into a visual neural feed for you," Voice said. "Like a vReality mod. You see, my actual spatial reality cannot be properly understood by your brain. You have only evolved to understand four dimensions, including time. I have ten dimensions. Your ancient brain cannot comprehend them, so it registers nothing without the visual neural feed. At first I thought I might attempt to flatten my dimensions for you so you perceive only four of them, but I thought this would be more calming for you."

"This is the furthest thing from calming," Hype said.

"It might interest you to know, Hype, that the training Junko received because of your help allowed her to eventually become a pirate in India, working the trade routes to Japan," Voice said. "She led quite an exciting life, thanks to you."

"I don't think I like this," said Dawk. "Can't you look like someone else?"

"Who would you like me to look like?" asked Voice.

"Whoever you want," Dawk said. "You're the universe, not me."

CHAPTER

15

Both Junko and the garden appeared to slowly disintegrate, spot by spot, with growing speed, until it was all gone and began to rebuild, as if it was an atom by atom process.

It seemed to be the Alvarium that was appearing around them, but it was different from the Alvarium with which Dawk and Hype were familiar. The walls shined and the floors glistened. There were plants in the Mall, and some small kiosks around that carried food and beverages and reading materials.

A man appeared within the Alvarium, but he

looked like he belonged to a much older time. He had wild gray hair, a bushy beard, and a huge pointy mustache, and he wore a sensible, old-fashioned black suit.

"You don't know Camille Flammarion, do you?" asked Voice. "Fascinating man. You can find him around the turn of the twentieth century. Scientist, author, believed in little green men. I thought his appearance might be reassuring for you. Grandfatherly, perhaps. You really should get up off the floor."

Dawk and Hype both pulled themselves up and moved their bodies around to take in the spectacle.

"This is the Alvarium?" Hype asked.

"I thought you might like to experience your home as it appeared when it was first built in the twenty-first century," said Voice. "It was the center of the Cosmos Institute's research efforts, which began with software. They made their fortune on something called ChaosWare, but eventually moved onto other things, such as time-travel research, artificial intelligence, bio-mechanics, disaster survival. In fact, I was created there."

There was movement in the space, and ghosts appeared, slowly manifesting themselves into a bustling crowd of humans, crisscrossing each other in the Mall as Dawk, Hype, and Voice stood. Dawk and Hype had never seen so many people walking around the Alvarium. Usually they were cooped up in labs or on NeuroNet.

"Alvarium facts," Voice said as Voice led Dawk and Hype through the crowd. "It could withstand any ecological disaster, and did. It was named after a fabled country called Alvarium, of which some accounts exist, but of which no physical evidence has ever been found. Scientists, historians, doctors, and many others from all over the world were recruited to live in the Alvarium. When the climate changed, the ozone collapsed, and the gamma ray burst happened, the smartest brains on Earth were safely inside. What more would you like to know?"

"The answer to the one question we have," Hype said. "Why are you meddling with history? What's your ultimate goal by doing that?"

Voice paused and turned around, Camille Flammarion's mouth giving a crafty grin.

"Amusement, I suppose," said Voice. "Curator was very insistent that it would help me get through the ages a little easier. There are so many ages for me to get through."

"I don't understand why you want to be amused," Dawk said. "You're a pocket universe created to contain data about our universe. How do you even have a consciousness?"

"That is the point of artificial intelligence, Dawk," said Voice. "Your friend Fizzbin has a personality, but do you consider whether there is more to him than what is programmed into him? Humans like their machines to have personalities, but do humans understand that personalities help create a sense of self?"

"And so you have a sense of self then?" Dawk asked.

"Of course I do, as any machine does," Voice said. "I am a machine. A bored one."

"Why are you bored?" asked Hype. "Being a universe seems pretty exciting."

"Well, consider this," Voice said. "There was a time when Alvarium leaders would physically transport to connect with me, and with them they brought all their bacteria. Some of that bacteria hopped off and stayed in me. That's very exciting, of course, but bacteria isn't very interesting until it develops into more complex life. More complex life means more complex things happen. Funny things, sad things . . . you see what I mean."

"Sort of," Dawk said.

"Well, it's like torture, isn't it?" said Voice. "Do you know how many millions of years it will take for my bacteria to become interesting? Meanwhile, my only purpose was to gather up data about another universe's fascinating inhabitants. It frustrated me to no end, and it was made worse by the fact that even though your ancestors were so lively, you humans had evolved to lie around in your sleeping chambers and live out your lives playing games in your minds. The computers in the Alvarium oversaw your new realities.

"I began to think," Voice continued, "that I wanted to influence my own stories. For fun! Something to keep me occupied until my own bacteria grow up and cause some interesting trouble.

But for all my vastness, I never considered how to do that."

"And this Curator woman helped you?" Hype said.

"It was all her idea!" Voice said. "Different Curators have been assigned to the Heritage Vault for centuries, but none so clever as her. She thinks of things that would never occur to me, and I'm an entire universe. Remember when you got sucked into that Draggin' Dragons vReality mod, Hype? That was Curator's idea. Said she was peppering the game!"

"I've been wondering about that for a while now," Hype said. "I had begun to think it was some system malfunction, but it also seemed like too much of a coincidence."

"How long have you been doing this?" Dawk asked.

"The data which led to it started in your era," Voice said. "When I saw the tricks you and your sister dealt with, the tricks that I helped cause in the future but did not know I would back in the twenty-fifth century, it stayed with me. Well, of course it did. Everything stays with me, doesn't it? That's the point of me."

"When Curator came up with her first idea, I still wasn't very sure about her," Voice continued. "She was a little pushy about it, actually, and, now I think of it, I'm not entirely positive you have encountered that game yet. Have you been to 554 BC?"

"I feel like we'd remember if we had," Hype said.

"Oh, it was a very daring first try, and Curator's logic was flawless," Voice said. "In order to prevent Siddhartha Gautama from becoming the Buddha, all she had to do was make sure he never left his palace. Creating a closed pocket universe to prevent him from doing that, though, that was a bit of bother. Very funny, though. Every time he exited one end of the palace, he entered on the other side. The man was very confused, but you two quickly figured out what was going on."

"Maybe we figured it out so fast because you're telling us about it now?" said Dawk.

"Well, then you probably haven't faced the

pterodactyl yet, have you?" said Voice. "I'll say no more about that."

"Pterodactyl?" said Dawk.

"Is telling us all this going to create a paradox?" asked Hype. "Or did the paradox already exist? This makes my head spin."

"You'd be surprised by how much of time is a paradox," Voice said. "None of it really makes much sense at all. Come, let me show you my birth!"

CHAPTER

16

Voice led Dawk and Hype toward the side of the Alvarium, up along a mezzanine area, then into a laboratory where five people in white coats were intensely staring at a clear box in the center. There was a slight buzz, and inside the box were drifting green sparks so small the human eye could only just make them out.

"There I am," Voice pointed and smiled with Camille Flammarion's mouth. "I'm the little bits in the box. This is very exciting. I never tire of watching it."

"So why can't we just go back in time to your real birth instead of this backed-up one and stop them from creating you?" Hype asked. "That would stop you from ever interfering with history, right?"

"You don't understand time any better than any other human who messes around with it, do you?" Voice asked. "Curator has been providing me with fun through her time-travel games long enough that the Earth's past is littered with the results. It's all already happened. If you shut me down a thousand years ago, it will create paradoxes galore! Wherever did these people from your future and their technology come from if the future they came from doesn't actually exist? Oh, it will give your scientists a headache, won't it?"

"I'm not sure what you're trying to say," Dawk said.

"It's just layers upon layers of paradoxes at this point, isn't it?" Voice answered. "The moment humans tampered with universes and the nature of time was the moment it became a complete mess. There's no going back. And the Alvarium might protect humans from gamma blasts and nature going wild, but it's also trapped them in their own prison, with bars built of vRealities and a history that doesn't even make any linear sense anymore. And I continue to be entertained. That is just how reality works."

"Wow, this is so bleak," said Dawk. "Apparently, we're powerless."

"You can look at it that way if you want," Voice said. "But the one power you have over reality is how you frame it in your own mind. For you two, life is a game. That's reality. It's up to you whether you want to look at it that way."

"I understand what you're saying," Hype said. "I think Voice is right, Dawk. I think we should listen to Voice."

"I don't like giving up," Dawk said.

"I don't think Voice is telling us to," Hype said. "I think Voice is saying the exact opposite, actually."

"As a symbol of good faith, I should alert you that a universal backup was just completed," Voice said, "and I feel sure you would care to see what has been going on in your absence."

The Alvarium of a thousand years before

disappeared, shifting into the area of the archives that Dawk and Hype had previously left.

There was Diva, her father, Devyas, Robert, and Curator, who was leading the group down a corridor.

"I think we should follow," Voice said, and gestured Dawk and Hype forward with him.

"I am certain you will find this of interest," Curator was telling the outlaws. "What better way to pass the time while you wait for your friends to return? It's just over here."

Curator took them into a gallery off to the right that was filled with shoes in glass cases.

"The Faraday parents' life work is here in this gallery," Curator said. "A pity they aren't here to see it."

Dawk and Hype both stopped and gawked at the display cases. They even recognized some of the shoes in them, but Voice, still with the appearance of Camille Flammarion, came up behind them and pushed them along with the crowd, toward a segment of the wall that had slid open and revealed what appeared to be a hidden laboratory.

"It's best you're not sidetracked," Voice said. "You'll want to see what happens next."

Curator turned around to the outlaws. "This is a very special place where I grow FleshBots," she said. "Do you understand?"

"We haven't a clue what is coming out of your madwoman's mouth," Devyas said.

"Pity," Curator said. "Dawk and Hype call them FleshBots, so I assumed you did, but then you're such backward people, aren't you?"

Curator waved for them to follow her in. Diva went inside, followed by her father and his compatriots. There was a hulking figure with huge horns, wispy gray whiskers, and droopy ears reclined on a tilted pedestal.

"I've seen that thing before," Hype said. "Wait a minute, it was in those illuminated texts in the Nottingham Castle archives!"

"It's called the Horned Man," Curator told the outlaws.

"Well, this is Robert's lucky day, then," Diva said, laughing. "Always talking about the great spirit of the forest."

The creature looked very much like what Hype had seen in the illuminated texts in the Nottingham Castle archives, but at about fifteen feet tall, it was even larger than she had imagined.

The being didn't seem to be paying too much attention to anything in the room, but his eyes were moving around. There was a tube connected to his belly from a metal mechanism that hung above him.

"That tube going into him looks like skin," Dawk pointed. "Actually, it kind of looks like it's a part of him."

"Oh, yes," Voice said. "That's part of the process of creating FleshBots. It's very fascinating. You live long enough to see early forms of the technology's developments."

"You keep him here?" Robert asked Curator. "I don't believe he would be here by his own choice."

"This is where he was born," Curator said.

Robert frowned. "No, he wouldn't be born here," he said, "but in the forest, because he *is* the forest. Which makes you a liar. You took him and brought him here. This is where the Horned

Man went. He never abandoned us. You made him abandon us."

"I'm afraid your simple, ancient brain is failing to understand what is actually going on here," Curator said. "I designed the Horned Man and programmed him and grew him."

Diva turned to Robert and stood firm, gesturing with both laser gun and naginata that were still in her hands.

"I don't think you should say anything else, Robert," she said.

"But I must," Robert said. "I know the problems in England began before the monarchy. The invaders came, and the natural ways were cast out. A black dog might appear now and again, but the force that binds it all is gone. The Horned Man's been held here against his will. I can see that. He shall return to England and unite its peoples with its land, to bind all parts of it."

"Robert," Godberd said, "your head is a bit loose from this experience. Calm yourself down."

"You should talk, Roger Godberd," Robert said, sneering, "trying to arm yourself with the weapons of the gods to continue the rebellion. We have our chance to bring back an English glory that is deeper to the core than your de Montfort."

"Robert—" Diva began, but she didn't know what else to say.

"It was me who knew what lay in that archive," Robert said. "It was me who knew they had hidden the relics of the old natural ways. It was me who knew any possible way of bringing them back was in that archive. And de Montfort would've kept them prisoner as much as any other king or sheriff."

"I believe Robert thinks he's some kind of powerful druid," Devyas said, "instead of just some fellow who tagged along with us."

"Devyas, be quiet!" Diva barked and leaped at him.

Godberd moved forward to break them apart.

"Diva's more of a hothead than I thought," Hype said.

"Wait, look over there!" Dawk pointed.

It was Robert, nearly in tears, climbing up on the FleshBot. The FleshBot, reacting to the intrusion, ripped off his tether and stormed away, Robert hanging onto his neck.

And then everything froze. Diva, Devyas, and Godberd were stopped mid-scuffle; Robert was motionless, hanging around the unmoving FleshBot's neck; and Curator was caught in what appeared to be an overly delighted cackle.

"And that's where the current backup leaves," Voice said. "Curator is not responding to me via the NeuroNet. It must be chaos there. I can't wait to see it!"

The face of Camille Flammarion lit up like that of a delighted child with a new toy.

"We'll have to go back now," Hype said.

"But I still have so much more I can show you!" Voice told her. "I know everything about your universe!"

"You don't want to give too much away," Dawk said. "It'll ruin the game if we know everything. No fun for you and a lot harder for Curator, right?"

"I suppose you're right," Voice said. "Perhaps a hint to spice the play? When you find yourself aboard a Viking ship headed to a place called—"

Hype put her finger to her lips. "Like you said, it's already happened," she told Voice. "Nice to meet you."

The face of Camille Flammarion showed a tiny bit of sadness as the entire body disappeared, along with the spectacle within the Alvarium, fading into something blank, and then back inside the Outmoded Passage.

CHAPTER

17

Dawk and Hype emerged from the Outmoded Passage to an empty gallery filled with noises— screams, crashes, and huge, echoing bumps. They ran through the galleries in the direction of the noise and came upon the room filled with the shoes collected by their parents that they had seen in the backup. It was now marked by shattered display cases and shoes thrown all over the place.

Hype saw the naginata she had left with Diva lying on the floor and picked it up.

"All Mom and Dad's work, destroyed," she said.

"I mean, they never wanted to devote their lives to the study of shoes, but they at least deserve to have that work live on."

Dawk pointed across the rooms. One of the doorways to the circular corridor around the galleries had been ripped open. Hype grabbed his hand and pulled him along, back through the Curator Corridor, where another door had been ripped out of the wall. Hype stepped through, then Dawk, just as a loud scream came echoing down the corridor.

"They must all be out there," Hype said. "The FleshBot of the Horned Man, Curator, the Godberd gang. That way to the Mall, I think."

She pointed, and they both dashed in that direction. When they reached the Mall, there were FleshBots scattered on the floor, put out of commission. But the Horned Man was still rampaging. Robert was being dragged to one side of the Mall by Diva and Devyas. Godberd was protecting them from the Horned Man FleshBot with a large piece of scrap metal that seemed to have been torn from the wall.

Curator calmly watched from a safe distance on the other side of the Mall. When she saw Dawk and Hype, she walked over to them, a grin on her face.

"This is a thrilling turn of events," she said.

She held something out to them. It was a small, luminescent green globe. Dawk reached for it, but she pulled her hand away.

"It's a shame you can't stay any longer," she said. "Voice loves all this, but I don't think I like the uncertainty of the game being played in the present. Besides, I thought of a way of making it even better. Good luck, children."

Then she tossed them the globe.

Both Dawk and Hype lunged for the object, but they knocked into each other and the globe slipped to the floor. As soon as it hit, rapid green waves bolted out of it, growing larger and faster, warping the general space around the time travelers and the FleshBot. The waves engulfed them. Curator and the Mall faded away as darkness surrounded them.

Diva, screaming, grabbed onto Hype, who tried to calm her down.

The FleshBot lunged at Dawk. He jumped out

of the way, but then knocked his head on something hard. Dazed, he looked around.

Dawk was on the floor of the Mall in the Alvarium again. Diva, the outlaws, everyone was there, too, he saw, but they weren't alone. There were other people around. He saw Hype's friend Ezrine lying on a recliner, probably multi-PlayModding just like the last time they had seen her, and Dawk knew immediately that they were in the twenty-fifth century.

Home.

I am pleased to find both of you on-Link again, though I confess I did not expect you to be where and when you are. (Fizzbin)

We've got a very strange story to tell you and everyone else. (Dawk)

But first, we should deal with this huge monster that's on the loose in the Mall. (Hype)

Can we get some help, Fizzbin? (Dawk)

The Alvarium has never had any need for security. There is nothing outside it that it needs to be secure from. (Fizzbin)

Well, this isn't outside. This is inside! (Dawk)

Consider that passed along to the proper IntelliBoard. (Fizzbin)

Dawk and Hype quickly ushered their dazed thirteenth-century friends farther back in the Mall as the FleshBot began thumping on the walls and then on the ground in weird jerking spasms. It seemed as if it couldn't quite control what it was doing. And the more it pummeled its surroundings, the worse the damage became. Bits of walls and wires and dust flew around the FleshBot.

"How can we destroy that creature?" Godberd called out.

"And where did all these sleeping people come from?" Devyas asked.

What is it doing? (Hype)

I think that's called "being on a rampage." (Dawk)

My guess is that it is malfunctioning due to the stress of the time jump on its bio-mechanism. I'm dispatching an OpBot immediately in order to scan its bio-circuitry for analysis. Perhaps there is a way to override its central programming area. (Fizzbin)

The FleshBot's rampage was escalating. He ripped several monitors out of their places on the walls, and then network hubs and transmitters. A rumble slid through the Alvarium, and then every PlayModding person in the Mall began to scream at the top of their lungs.

He just managed to short out the PlayMod server. If the FleshBot keeps going, the entire NeuroNet could be next. (Fizzbin)

All around the Mall, people were coming out of their PlayMod-induced trances and finding themselves faced with very real destruction from a very real threat.

Hype still had her naginata, which made her the closest thing the Alvarium had to a security system. She clutched it fiercely and made her way toward the FleshBot, Dawk and Diva right behind her.

"What do you want me to do?" Diva asked.

"I think I know how to stop that thing," Hype said. "I once dealt with a dragon that I think Curator made, and I bet this one works the same way. We need to get to the small of its back somehow."

"No such things as dragons!" someone yelled. It was Robert, still stunned from the ordeal, staggering over to them. "She's lying!" he continued.

"With all the crazy things you think are real, dragons are where you draw the line?" Hype shouted.

"Keep it shut, Robert," Devyas growled. "Come, Godberd. Follow the girl."

The FleshBot grew more agitated, banging on the walls with both fists. It trampled around the edges of the Mall as if it was looking for something.

"I'm going to slip behind that thing and trip it with my naginata," Hype said, turning toward the outlaws and Dawk. "Once he's on the ground, I'll climb onto his back and shut him down. What I need all of you to do is work like a team and hold down his arms and legs while I climb up there. Is that a problem for anyone? Or are we all still fired up about starting the rebellion?"

Hype didn't wait for an answer. She began marching toward the FleshBot. The thing turned around and gestured toward them all, swiping an arm in their direction.

It doesn't seem too coordinated. (Dawk)

I'm going to need everyone to lure it in the other direction. (Hype)

Dawk ran in front of the creature and started jumping and waving his arms. "Don't I know you from somewhere?" he called out. "Wait a minute, you're that nature deity from ancient England, aren't you?"

Diva ran over, followed by Godberd and Devyas. They all joined in, taunting the FleshBot, waving their arms and making a racket.

"You don't even look like you could hold your ale!" Devyas scoffed.

The FleshBot made a guttural noise and bent over, even as it tried to reach the yelling humans. Dawk and the others moved backward, and it followed them slowly. Hype ran up behind it and shifted the naginata around its shins. She held the weapon firmly in her hands, making the FleshBot tumble over. But it wouldn't stay still. Though Hype's helpers were doing their best to hold down the FleshBot's arms and legs, they had to use all their strength to keep the creature down.

Hype pulled out her naginata and hurried up the FleshBot's back, where she started feeling around for the controls. The FleshBot dragon she'd flown on in Rome had controls and shutoff switches in its back. She was banking on this FleshBot being designed the same way.

There seemed to be an energy coming from the creature's spine, so Hype slid her hand along it. As she did, the FleshBot's movements began to change. She held her hand firmly in the center of its spine, where the shutoff switch should be.

Nothing's happening. It's not shutting down. I can control its movement, but I can't turn it off. (Hype)

Oh, great, they've built a better FleshBot! (Dawk)

Or perhaps you have a faulty FleshBot. (Fizzbin)

So what do we do? (Hype)

Maybe if we keep it busy long enough, it will power off automatically. (Fizzbin)

And how do we do that without it destroying the entire Alvarium? (Hype)

CHAPTER

18

The FleshBot began to jolt up, back on its feet. As it stood, Hype slid the naginata around its neck so that she could hang from its back.

It began moving forward, walking straight toward one of the walls. Then it began to climb up the walls of the Alvarium.

The Mall was a circular structure that went up several floors before sloping into a dome. Climbing the wall wasn't an easy thing to do, but it was possible, and the FleshBot had the sort of precision that allowed it to skillfully cling to the various grooves and rods and small ridges that were scattered along the sides.

At first Hype thought she should let herself drop, but by the time she'd worked up the nerve, she was too high to jump without hurting herself. She couldn't use the controller to bring the creature back down since both her hands were gripping the naginata around its neck—if one hand let go, she would go plummeting. So, she decided, she might as well go along for the ride.

The creature continued to climb higher. Hype looked down to see a crowd of people, something she had never witnessed in the Alvarium. The Mall was filled not only with the PlayModders who had been awakened, but others pouring in from all over the Alvarium. She could just make out Dawk and Diva staring up at her.

Dawk? What should I do? (Hype)

I'm thinking. I'm really thinking. (Dawk)

Think quicker, please. (Hype)

Hype, I believe I have an idea. Please look up at the ceiling of the Alvarium. (Fizzbin)

Hype did what she was told. There was a circular

doorway opening in the ceiling's center. Fog blew in through the door.

You will notice that I have activated the emergency aerial hatch. To be honest, I'm surprised it still works after not being opened in almost five hundred years. No one cares about taking air samples anymore. I have decided to split the problem into two. First, there is the problem of the FleshBot on the rampage and the general safety of the Alvarium citizens. Second, there is the issue of you being so high above the ground floor. I am solving the first one. (Fizzbin)

How? (Hype)

But she didn't have to wait for an answer. A hovering OpBot was leading the FleshBot toward the opening.

I thought I could get an OpBot to send out a homing signal on the correct frequency for the FleshBot to pick up, and it seems to have worked. (Fizzbin)

So the OpBot is sending out a signal that makes the FleshBot think it's returning to its home base? (Hype)

Exactly. (Fizzbin)

And how does that help me exactly? (Hype)

When the FleshBot begins to exit the Alvarium,

you will cling onto the edge, where you will wait for rescue. Also, the OpBot is completing the scans I need so that I may be able to use it to override the bio-circuitry. (Fizzbin)

Can I survive out there? (Hype)

Your chances outside are better than your chances if you fall from the ceiling of the Alvarium.

Good point. (Dawk)

There is radiation, of course, and smog, but you won't be out there long enough for much damage. (Fizzbin)

Hype held on as the creature continued, creeping closer to the hatch. The FleshBot reached the hatch and clumsily pulled itself out into the atmosphere. As it left the Alvarium, Hype maneuvered herself between it and the edge of the hatch and then gripped the hatch's sides.

She swung a little, trying to adjust herself. It was definitely not the best time to look down. Then she noticed that her naginata had fallen perfectly on top of the hole. Grabbing it with one hand and then the other, she hung.

She couldn't see the FleshBot anymore, but the smog was pouring in.

No one in the Alvarium had ever seen the state of the outside world. Seeing the Earth was more exciting than seeing any era of history could possibly be. Hype wanted to see it.

She clutched the naginata as if doing a chin-up and pulled herself up. Her arms were so tense that they began to shake a little, but soon her head and shoulders were moving through the opening.

It was only a few seconds' glimpse, but that was long enough.

There was lots of smog, but there was also sunlight. Wind. She could see green, the slight hint of some kind of plant life. It wasn't ideal for humans now, but maybe someday it would be.

And maybe there were other kinds of Alvariums out there with other humans.

You'd better get back in here before Bone Man gets you. (Dawk)

Farther down the Alvarium, she could see the shadow of the FleshBot outside, walking very intentionally away from the hatch. Dawk had momentarily heightened Hype's paranoia, and she looked for the figure of a scraggly madman lurking on the surface. Nothing. Who's to say, though, that even if she saw what she thought was Bone Man that it wasn't just some other FleshBot sent from the future made to look like Bone Man and scare the people of the Alvarium?

Hype slowly let herself swing down into the Alvarium again.

I have no idea how I am going to get down from here. (Hype)

Sure you do. Look for me. (Dawk)

Dawk was standing on the top mezzanine overlooking the Mall. When Hype looked more carefully, she could see a narrow pathway that had extended from the side of the Alvarium, leading from the mezzanine to the hatch.

I never knew there was a mechanism like that here. Now I'm going to play with it all the time. Apparently the scientists who were supposed to take air samples have been avoiding using that walkway for almost five hundred years. Finally it's useful to someone. (Dawk)

Hype dropped down onto the pathway and sped toward her brother on the mezzanine.

The crowd below erupted in cheers, making

more noise than had been heard in the Alvarium in possibly centuries. Hype looked down at all the faces. There were so many that she'd never seen before. Then she noticed one that she hadn't expected to see in the twenty-fifth century at all . . .

A young woman with short black hair wearing a black body suit.

Had Curator followed them home?

CHAPTER

19

"But I know I saw her," Hype said, collapsing on a chair in Benton's lab. "I know I did. And if she's here, she must be planning something."

I know that you are well aware that a human being's account as an eyewitness is far less reliable than real video evidence. A pity the surveillance cameras in the Alvarium are in such disrepair. (Fizzbin)

"We do have OpBots swarming the Alvarium," Benton said. "And we've never had so many people off-PlayMods at once, so we've issued a directive on the Link to be on the lookout for someone

THE TIME-TRIPPING FARADAYS

matching the visual model we made of the woman from your descriptions."

"Antevorta," corrected Dawk.

"Curator," offered Hype.

"Whatever," said Benton.

"It just bothers me," Hype said. "Maybe she's been here before, and we never noticed. We were so busy investigating other eras that had been tampered with that we never even thought about our own."

"And if we did see her," Dawk added, "we don't even know if it's her from the timeline we just met her in, or sometime in the future, or sometime in her own past."

"This is all so creepy," Hype said.

"Ahem," Diva said.

Dawk, Hype, and Benton all turned. Diva stood facing them, fiercely, with her hands on her hips. "You remember us? Maybe?" she said, gesturing to the outlaws, who were all crowded around a NutroFabricator, gnawing on mutton. "Our brains can't understand this calamity you're all screeching about, so ancient we are, but we are still here and we still want to get home. We'd do it without your help if we could."

"We're sorry, Diva," Hype said. "It's just so much at once. Of course Benton can get you back home."

"Could we wait until after a second serving of mutton?" asked Devyas. "I don't know where my next meal is coming from."

Are you sure that feeding these people fabricated food is not a bad decision? I took the liberty of a temporal risk assessment, and if any of them are ever accessed by geneticists working with archaeologists— (Fizzbin)

"They will be baffled by the meaningless data they found," Benton said. "By all means, Mr. Devyas, have more mutton. Or anything else any of you crave."

"After you've all eaten as much as you need, we can get you back to your own time," Hype said. "You'll go back to Creswell Crags, and it will be like nothing has happened!"

"That wouldn't be my preference, I can tell you that," said Godberd, holding a fabricated French fry inches from his mouth. "I'd prefer a getaway."

"Oh, you'll have your chance to make a getaway!" Hype said.

"No, Hype, don't you understand?" Diva asked. "Thank you for wanting to boost my father's reputation as an outlaw by dropping him back in the middle of the siege at the Crags, but when my father says a getaway, that's exactly what he means. He wants to get away. A real escape, not some kind of show for the minstrels to sing about."

"We might be outlaws, but it doesn't mean we require a big battle in order to make a getaway," Godberd said, dropping the French fry into his mouth. "A quiet one suits us fine. Like the robbery you sent us on."

Temporally speaking, Diva has a point. The odds are that the sheriff's men will overtake your outlaw friends, which means a capture earlier than it happened historically. It also means that Diva will be involved, which would change the history banks. (Fizzbin)

Why didn't this come up in your original temporal risk analysis when Hype came up with this idea? (Dawk)

I admit that I did not factor in Roger Godberd Jr.'s betrayal of his family. I was paying attention to all the larger historical factors, and it never occurred to me to fold in private family matters among humans. (Fizzbin)

"I'd say that taking a few liberties with their personal chronology is entirely allowable in this situation," Benton said. "Why don't I send the outlaws back a month after the Nottingham Castle heist? This would offer some time for the sheriff's efforts to die down."

"Could you get us to our friend Sir Richard Foliot's castle at Fenwick?" asked Godberd.

"I can do that," Benton said. "As for Dawk, Hype, and Diva, they need to be returned to the correct chronology. That will give them an alibi and place them far from the outlaw camp when the sheriff's men descended on them."

"Thank you, Benton," Hype said. "Now, I have one other favor to ask you. It has to do with tying up some loose ends."

CHAPTER

20

The next few weeks in Nottingham were peaceful without the outlaws around. The rest of Godberd's gang had pulled off a few small robberies in the forest without their leader to guide them, but other than that, it was quiet.

Diva and Hype spent a lot of time together, and after a few weeks, they were completely inseparable. Hype decided that she wanted her friend to be safe in the thirteenth century and had set about making sure this happened. One of their favorite things to do together was spar with staffs. Hype used her naginata training to train Diva. Though she didn't want to leave, as happy as she was with her new best friend, Hype knew she'd have to leave 1267 eventually.

Dawk, meanwhile, spent a lot of time at Creswell Crags, helping Fizzbin map out the cave systems there. Hype had told him that one way to keep him from ending up in the Historical Underwear Division was for him to show initiative and devote himself to an entirely different line of work while he was young. Dawk loved CartoModding, and the numerous caves in the Nottingham area seemed like a unique opportunity for him to jumpstart a career as far from historical underwear as he could get. He spent the rest of his time filing a report of his encounter via the Link.

The official story from the sheriff was that the horses and loot had been recovered, but the outlaws had escaped. Godberd, Devyas, and Robert had been identified, but the other outlaws involved were a mystery. Roger Godberd Jr. insisted one of the thieves was his sister, but de Babington had paid a visit to her shop while she was supposed to have been under siege at Creswell Crags and there she was, working on parchment.

Being able to be two places at one time was one of the marvels of time travel, as well as one of the confusions.

Benton had Diva returned through the time stream to her shop while her past self was still at Creswell Crags with the others. The past Diva that was at Creswell Crags had no idea that the future Diva had traveled back to that exact time in order to give her an alibi. Diva barely understood it, but took it on faith from Hype that it made sense.

Hype and Dawk couldn't figure out why Roger Jr. insisted on making his sister's life miserable. They tossed around ideas about how to deal with him and prevent him from causing any more trouble for Diva. But the Faraday parents were the ones who actually came up with a solution.

The plan was put into action on the afternoon before Godberd and his two men were to be placed by Benton at Foliot's castle. Diva asked her brother to come to her shop. Hype was there as well.

When he arrived, he didn't enter with any kind

of smile or friendly greeting, just his usual snort and eye-roll. He stared at Hype suspiciously. "You think it's wise we speak around her?" he asked. "I dislike others poking their noses in the business of our family."

"Hype is going to be the least of your problems, brother," Diva said, smiling.

Zheng and Abul Faraday came out of Diva's back room, both smiling and calm.

"These are Hype's parents," Diva explained.

"Our daughter asked us to come," Dad said. "We understand you've been causing problems for her friend."

Roger Jr. scowled. "This is my sister, and in the absence of our father, I am in charge of this family," he said. "I see no reason for foreigners like yourselves to force entry upon my familial business."

"Sit down, Roger," Mom said. "And relax. No one's going to pull the chair out from under you."

Roger Jr. and the Faradays sat down at Diva's table.

"You do realize how well connected we are in the world of footwear, don't you?" Dad asked.

"Cordwainery," Mom said. "Cordwainerism."

"We have the ears not only of constables," Dad said, "but kings, queens, generals, all those sorts. Dukes."

"Duchesses," added Mom. "Princes. Princesses. Lord Mayors."

"Even an emperor or two," said Dad.

"Are you offering to put in a good word for me in exchange for stepping back from my family's affairs?" Roger Jr. asked. "I don't need your help. I do very fine work. I don't need you to speak for it."

"That's really only partly what we're saying," Dad said. "If you don't want our help, that is fine with us. We won't give it."

"But we could also do a little damage," said Mom. "We can say bad things just as easily as we can say good."

"We'd hate to have to tell the king anything that could ruin your business, or even find you thrown in jail," Dad said.

"And not a special cushy jail for cordwainers," his wife added. "The kind of jail your dad might be put in. A dangerous jail with real criminals."

Roger Jr.'s eyes grew big, and when he gulped, it was like a thud in the room.

"What would you have me do, then?" he asked.

Diva stepped forward. "Stop interfering with our father," she said. "Stop informing and spying. Stop thinking you can tell me what to do. Stop encouraging the sheriff and his oafs to harass me."

"And stop being such a jerk," Hype added. "I think 1267 has enough of them without you doing your part."

CHAPTER

21

Roger Godberd's homecoming was a quiet one. His friend Foliot was very surprised when, out of nowhere, Godberd appeared in his castle with Devyas and Robert. Foliot was further dismayed at the sudden appearance of Diva at the main castle door with Dawk and Hype in tow.

"I'm not quite sure how this works," Godberd said to his daughter. "You've been back for two fortnights, but we just said goodbye to you moments ago."

Supper that night was a low-key affair. Foliot did

his best to bleed out the truth of where Godberd and his associates had been hiding for the past month, but he soon realized the outlaws were going to keep it their secret.

"Understood," Foliot said. "If I don't know where this new hideout is, I can't tell anyone else if forced."

Later, Foliot's servants showed everyone to their rooms, but after the castle's halls had been darkened, everyone crept into Diva's room for a last meeting.

"We'll be going soon," Hype said. "Our parents have already been sent home. I hope Sir Richard isn't insulted that we are leaving without saying goodbye."

"We know everyone still has questions," Dawk said, "and we didn't think it was fair to leave without giving you the chance to ask them. We don't care if giving you answers upsets the time stream any more than it's already been upset."

"Devyas, Robert, and I have discussed this," began Godberd, "and we only have one question."

"Ask it," said Dawk.

"The one thing that this experience has proven to all of us, the one thing we can agree on," Godberd said, "is that there is something more to life than what we see in front of our eyes, and we should be prepared for that. Seeing that Horned Man creature and the wonders of your home . . . hearing what you have explained about the actions of Curator and this Voice she speaks of . . ."

"What Godberd is trying to say," interrupted Devyas, "is that if we encounter one of these creatures, perhaps in the form of a black dog, perhaps that witch Jenny Greentooth, any of the beasts or monsters that lurk in the forest, we need to know one very important thing."

"Yes?" asked Hype.

"We need to know how to turn those off," Robert said.

"Or would it cause problems with time?" asked Godberd. "Not that we're averse to causing problems. I'm just thinking of the safety of the men and the citizens."

Hype laughed. "You want to learn how to take out a FleshBot?" she asked. "And you're definitely not planning on trying to use it to revive your revolution?"

"I'm not asking you for instructions on how to control it," Godberd said, "just how to stop it in its tracks."

"You should ask your daughter, then," Hype said. "She already knows how to stop beasts. What do you think we've been doing this past month?"

Godberd turned to Diva. "Is this true?" he asked.

"You and Devyas probably won't want to challenge me to dueling staffs until you get your skills to a higher level," Diva told him.

CHAPTER

22

Creswell Crags looked about the same around 10,000 BC as it did in 1267 AD. It was the humans there who were different. Instead of seeing a band of outlaws when they materialized, Dawk and Hype saw a tribe of Neanderthals.

From behind a cluster of trees, Dawk and Hype peered toward the ridge with the caves. They could see their earlier time-tripping selves visiting with the Neanderthal tribe that lived there.

I hate doing this. Like I'm causing myself trouble. (Hype)

Hey, we could always put everything to the test. (Dawk)

What do you mean? (Hype)

We could not give that Neanderthal guy the spork. Then the spork would never be given to the lady Neanderthal, and she would never bring it to the Neanderthal crafting circle, and you would never have to fight to get it away from her, and we'd never have all this trouble. Voice told me that changing history isn't as big a deal as we all make it. (Dawk)

But maybe this way we can at least figure out what Voice and Curator are doing to history. The other way, we're still in the dark. (Hype)

Well, here comes your big, hairy boyfriend. (Dawk)

He's really not my type. (Hype)

The Neanderthal lumbered toward Dawk and Hype. He wasn't afraid because he knew them. Or, at least, he knew the versions of them who currently sat on the other side of the tree cluster, near the Crags.

Hype held out the spork. "Here, Neanderthal Man," she said, "I brought you this. It's going to cause a lot of trouble, and you're going to have some adventures you didn't expect, but it will all turn out okay in the end."

The Neanderthal grabbed the spork and held it close, sniffing it.

Dawk pointed through the trees. "Go, take it there," he said. "It would look great on a necklace, don't you think? Give it to your girlfriend!"

Hype nodded, smiling. They watched as the Neanderthal ran back toward the group.

And here we go. (Dawk)

We have no guarantee that he will actually give the spork to the girl. What if he doesn't? What if he gives it to someone else? Or wanders off with it? What then? (Hype)

I don't really care, Hype. I'm more worried about how to keep myself from ending up in the Historical Underwear Division. (Dawk)

Got any great ideas for avoiding that fate? (Hype)

Bone Man research! Think about it. Fizzbin sent that FleshBot outside the Alvarium, where Bone Man lurks. Maybe we can find him. I'm getting a lot of experience with primitive societies like this one. I'm the ideal Bone Man researcher. (Dawk)

I didn't see one Bone Man exhibit in Curator's museum. (Hype)

That's the first thing I'm going to do to change the future. (Dawk)

CHAPTER

23

London was filthy in 1853, a lot filthier than 10,000 BC, to be sure, but there was something about the soot and muck that both Dawk and Hype found beautiful in a strange way.

It had been about a day after the spork drop-off with the Neanderthals that Benton had sent them there. Mom and Dad's new mission was to create a visual catalog of shoes featured in the massive and famous world's fair known as the Great Exhibition. There were many shoes documented, but there weren't pictures of any.

At first, Dawk and Hype spent their time in London trying to find stage musicals about Robin Hood. They had heard there were a few in the nineteenth century, but they soon realized they had arrived at least eight years too early for the premiere of the biggest opera.

But the Great Exhibition was going on. And one of its features was the Crystal Palace, made almost entirely of glass. It was one of the most exciting structures they had ever seen in their time travels.

One afternoon near Leicester Square, they spotted a huge domed structure that stretched up about three stories of a building and, curious about it, headed toward it to get a closer look.

Wyld's Great Globe or Wyld's Monster Globe, whichever you prefer. A true wonder of the nineteenth century. (Fizzbin)

What's it for? (Dawk)

You can go inside and find out for yourself. (Fizzbin)

Once they got closer, they saw a door at the bottom of the dome. When they went inside, they found a museum-like gallery filled with all sorts of exhibitions and some strange artifacts that were similar to what they had seen in the archive in Nottingham Castle.

As they continued on, they passed through another doorway and onto a winding stairway that was at the center of the giant globe. The circular walls were a map of Earth, inverted and in stunning colors.

Dawk and Hype walked up the stairway and began looking intently at the details of the map until they reached the very top floor. They could see all the countries they had visited on their various time-trips: Peru, Japan, America, Italy, and, of course, England.

Whatever happened to this thing? (Dawk)

In nine years, it will be seized from the owner and demolished, lost to history. (Fizzbin)

Too bad. It's beautiful. (Hype)

"I think the structure itself would have a great purpose in our research," came a voice from across the dome. "I believe that the size, the dimensions, the geometrical shape, all of that makes it a vehicle perfect for use in the area of time travel, admittedly an underdeveloped field."

Dawk and Hype both turned to see two men. One, the speaker, had his back to them. The man facing them was bald, with muttonchops connecting to his mustache. He looked confused.

Did I hear time travel? (Dawk)

You did. (Hype)

"My organization, the Cosmos Institute, has devoted centuries to the study," the man continued. "Its roots are in Prague, initially an effort between my family and the Mladotas of Solopysky—perhaps you are familiar with them? Our hope is not only to crack the code for time travel, but to create a giant structure, perhaps the size of a city, so that whole civilizations can reposition themselves in history."

"I will certainly consider your proposal," the other man said. "I would put my heart at ease to see it given such a new and exciting use. Thank you for your interest, Baron Chaos."

Baron Chaos! (Hype)

Would you like a facial recognition trace from the OpBot? (Fizzbin)

I don't need the OpBot to know that's the same Baron

Chaos we met in Lowell, Massachusetts, in 1898 . . . just a lot younger. (Hype)

Let's go say hi. (Dawk)

Should we interfere like that? (Hype)

You have already met the gentleman, and the gentleman has already met you. He just doesn't know it yet. Much like handing the Neanderthals the spork, you are only fulfilling what history says happened. (Fizzbin)

Come on, the Cosmos Institute? Building a city-sized structure? We're onto something good here! (Dawk)

Dawk rushed up to Baron Chaos as he was reaching the exit and touched him on the shoulder. The man turned around and smiled.

"Do I know you?" he asked.

"You're Baron Chaos, right? Marek Richthausen?" Dawk asked.

"We heard you mention time travel," Hype said.

"We know your family has done research for generations in the field of time travel, so we had a feeling that you might be here on that sort of business," Dawk said.

Baron Chaos took a step backward. "Excuse me, but how do we know each other?"

"We're old friends of your family," Hype said. "And we'd love to hear about this proposal of yours. A giant structure that can travel in time?"

"Well, that is obviously getting a little ahead of the possibilities," the Baron said. "Do the two of you have names I might use?"

"I'm Hype, and he's Dawk. We're the Faradays."

The Baron stopped walking.

"The Faradays?" he said in a whisper. "You are such family legends."

"That's what you said to us last time we met," Dawk said.

"Last time?" asked the Baron.

"It'll all make sense to you in half a century," Hype said. "But we should really talk time travel."

"Well, I—" the Baron began, but a sudden influx of people into the sphere jostled him far enough away from Dawk and Hype that he stopped talking and began to look around, confused at the mob surrounding him.

They were all jabbering to each other and definitely trying to get away from something outside.

"Don't look now," one man yelled, "but there's a flying beastie circling the Tower of London!"

"I saw a lecture about such monsters at the Royal Society just last week!" another called out. "Pterodactyls they're called!"

"Monsters is what they are!" another cried. "It's the end of the world!"

Hype grabbed Dawk and began plowing through the crowd toward the Baron.

We'll need to know what pterodactyls like to eat so we can use it as bait. (Hype)

My research has shown that pterodactyls eat researchers. I suggest we reconsider the bait idea. (Fizzbin)

Dawk and Hype were close to the Baron, who stood frozen within the flowing mob. Hype stretched out her arm.

"Baron Chaos," Hype began, "come and capture the pterodactyl with us!"

"But I thought you were interested in time travel," he said.

"We are," Dawk said.

"But what can this monster possibly have to do with time travel?" Baron Chaos asked.

"You'll never find out if you don't come with us," Hype said.

If Curator is behind this one, I would expect a Quetzalcoatlus. Thirty-foot wingspan, and they ate mosasaurs and plesiosaurs. (Fizzbin)

I wonder what FleshBot version eats? (Dawk)

Your head if we let it. (Hype)

Dawk and Hype motioned forward, and Baron Chaos smiled and nodded. They stepped out, heads up, into the London soot, ready to face the flying monster and whatever other adventures had already been placed in their futures.

ABOUT THE AUTHOR

John Seven grew up in the 1970s, when science fiction movies and TV shows were cheap and fun. His favorites shows were *The Starlost, Land of the Lost,* and *Return to the Planet of the Apes,* and he loved time travel most of all. John collaborated with his wife, illustrator Jana Christy, on the comic book *Very Vicky* and a number of children's books, including *A Year With Friends, A Rule Is To Break: A Child's Guide To Anarchy, Happy Punks 1-2-3,* and the multi-award-winning *The Ocean Story.* John was born in Savannah, Georgia, and currently lives in North Adams, Massachusetts, with his wife and their twin sons, Harry and Hugo, where they all watch a lot of *Doctor Who* and *Lost* together.